I0761783

Talk To Me

By Donna M. Zadunajsky

Talk To Me

"HELP ME!" series Book 2

This novel is a work of fiction.
Names, characters, places and incidents are either the product of the author's imagination or are used fictitiously. Any resemblance to actual persons, living or dead, events, or locales is entirely coincidental.

ISBN: 978-1541098442 (13) - Print
ISBN: 1541098447 (10) – Print
ISBN: 978-1-938037-63-4 - ebook

http://www.donnazadunajsky.com
http://www.facebook.com/donnamzadunajsky
http://twitter.com/72Zadunajsky
http://www.goodreads.com/72allshookup

Dedication

To all the lonely souls in the world.

You're not alone...

1 | Truth

If you had the power to stop something from happening, would you do it? I mean bad things, of course; no one would stop the good things from happening to them or someone else. Okay, maybe someone else, if you wanted the boy to yourself and didn't want to see the other girl happy, but that's not what this story is about.

This story has to do with more than a boy. It has to do with what I did to myself and what my best friend did. It's about trying to feel like me again, which I know will never happen, and definitely will not happen for my best friend, either. Besides, I'm too far gone to be saved; at least, I think I am.

The only thing I can do is tell you my story and have you decide if I'm worth saving. If I'm worth the oxygen I breathe, that you breathe.

Here's what you need to know about me before I start. I just turned fifteen this past September. I have two sisters, which I'll tell you more about them once I get into my story. Like most kids I know, both of our parents work, although my mom is the sole provider; not that there's anything wrong with that, it's just that my dad chose a different occupation. He works for children services, finding kids a good home.

So, before I get off-track on the real reason I want to tell my story, I have to say that there are some graphic images I'm about to share with you; so if you're one of those people that gets grossed out by sickening reality, then it's probably best you're reading this book and not watching a *vid.*

There will be sad parts and times when you wish you could reach into the book and save or hurt someone, but you can't, and not that I wouldn't want you to, it's just not always possible to save everyone. Besides, *my story* has already played out. By knowing about me, maybe it can keep this from happening to someone else or help you to see what is going on right in front of you?

Wouldn't that be something if we could actually save people? Keep them from getting hurt? Do you think that they would in-turn do the same for you? Then maybe this world wouldn't be such a bad place after all, if only people would stop being so cruel and hurtful to one another.

I mean, really, what is the point in hurting other people? Does it give them a high? Does it make them feel more superior? Is it their lot in life to see just how many people they can destroy?

See, I knew I'd get off-track about what I wanted to tell you. Just know this, when all is said and done, you'll know my story.

I hope that if this were to happen to you or anyone you know that reading this would save them—help them in some way. Because let's face it, we all need saving at some point in our lives…

2|School
Monday

You would think that in high school, life would be easy. That it would be the most fun you'll ever have in your life before the stress of being an adult takes over.

The friends you make will be there beside you through the rest of your life. You'll go to parties together. Graduate together. Possibly, even go to the same college together. But that would be getting ahead of ourselves. None of that is a guarantee in life. Every single one of us will graduate and go off into the world, whether it is college or some lousy job that we take just so we can pay the bills. But that's not my point here. That's not the reason for this story or what it's about.

Just like most of the kids I go to school with, I haven't figured out what I want to do with my life—more or less, think about next week or next month. These things float in my mind when I'm in some of my classes at school. Honestly, I would just be glad to pass the biology test tomorrow.

Speaking of biology, my teacher Mr. Herman says, "Study, study, study if you want to pass my tests. I'm not going to make it easy on you guys because LIFE. ISN'T. EASY."

Blah, blah, blah. "Whatever," I mumble under my breath when he makes that speech. Like biology even matters unless you're going to be a scientist or something. Who cares?

Finally, the bell rings, I gather my books, and head out the door before anyone else. I quickly weave my way through the hall as it starts to fill with other freshman students like me.

The building is an old historic building and only us freshman go to school here. There's a separate building for 10th, 11th, and 12th graders, where I and everyone else will go next year. *Awesome!* I'm so looking forward to it. That's sarcasm, if you didn't know.

I spin the lock on my locker and open it, throwing my books inside and grabbing what I need for after lunch. Before I can close the door, Mick Connors slams it for me; luckily, my hand wasn't still inside.

"What the hell?" I shout at him. "You just missed my hand, you ass." Knowing he really doesn't care.

I met Mick last year in eighth grade after I found out that he was a *cutter*. It wasn't like it was plastered all over the school or anything. I knew him from Shawn Bowers and Layla Manning.

Layla and I aren't like friends or anything; she's more Mick's friend than mine, or she used to be his friend.

Mick didn't have to tell me that she was the one who went to the school about what he was doing to himself; it was obvious it was her by the way they hung around each other. I mean, they ended up as girlfriend and boyfriend after he got help.

It's not that she was wrong for telling the school, but she could've, I don't know, maybe gone about it a different way. I also think there's more to the story then him just cutting himself.

As far as I can tell, he doesn't cut anymore. I remember him wearing long sleeves last year, and I had even seen cuts on the inside of his legs in PE class. Now he's been wearing short sleeves, and I see no cuts on his arms, just scars. *Good for him, he's found a reason to live*, I think to myself. *I wish I could.*

"Come on, Carly, now you're calling me names?" Mick says, grinning.

I smile, cause it's just how we are around each other. "Well, if the shoe fits," I reply, laughing. Mick and I started hanging out more the past two weeks. We've always sort of been friends, but since my *once forever* best friend stabbed me in the back, we hang around each other more now.

Mick and I get into step, walking side by side to the cafeteria. I used to sit with Bailey, but God she's like so much DRAMA—I can't stand her, so now I sit with Mick and Alisha, who pretty much keeps to herself.

Alisha talks to us, but it's not like we're best friends or anything like that. We don't share our inner most secrets. We don't hang out. Actually, I have to be honest with you; I really don't have a best friend. Well, I did two weeks ago, but she's a bitch and a trader, and she's not a friend I want to have if she doesn't care about me like I once did about her. It's probably better that way because if everything goes as planned on Saturday, I won't be here much longer.

* * *

Lunch blows by quickly, and so does the rest of my classes after lunch. Now, I'm gathering whatever books I need for home, and make my way to the buses outside.

It's stupid, yet smart, how they have the bus routes set up. If I miss this bus, it'll leave and go to the high school down the road a few blocks; then comes back here to pick up anyone who might have missed the bus the first time around. Told you it didn't make sense, but at the same time, it does.

Twenty minutes later, I'm stepping off the bus and walking up my driveway to the front door. Both my parents are at work so it's like I get the whole house to myself, for a while anyway.

I have an older sister Kyra who is eighteen and just started college, and I have a younger sister Rosie who is in second grade. She was more of an oops, so to speak. After like seven years and then oops, here comes another baby. Don't get me wrong, I do love my baby sis, but she can also get on my nerves at the same time too.

Once I get inside the house, I make my way to the kitchen and grab a juice box before going to my room. I know Rosie will be home in an hour so I have to finish what homework I can before she arrives.

I drop my bookbag on the floor of my bedroom and go into my parent's bedroom. I have to do this when they're not home because, well, if I was to get caught stealing from my mom's prescription bottle when she was home, then there would be a lot of questions. Truth is, I don't have those answers.

I open the drawer to my mom's nightstand and pick up the bottle of pills. I'm not sure why she has a bottle of Xanax, but hey, I'm not going to question it. One can only assume the kind of job she does can be stressful. That's why I'd never be a lawyer.

So, a couple of times a week, I come in and steal a few pills. I can't do it every day or she'd know some were missing.

I head back to my bedroom and open the door to my closet. In the far back, on the top shelf, I have a box. The box contains things that mean the world to me. Like pictures and small gifts that were given to me from friends or family members. Things I want to treasure for as long as I live; which like I said before, if all goes well that will end on Saturday.

I guess your question would be: *Why do I want to end my life?* I'm only fifteen—life has just begun. I should be out there living it up and having fun with my friends. But to be honest, life really sucks for me.

Okay, so maybe I should start from the beginning and tell you what happened lately that has made me think death would be a better choice. Because the truth is, life is full of shit! Some people make life out to be something so great and fulfilling, but for me, NO! It just sucks all-the-way-around. These are not the best years of our lives. Whoever said that is full of shit! Being a teenager is so much worse than being an adult, where at least you get some control over what happens to you.

There's so much stress with schoolwork, friends, boys and family stuff that it makes me want to throw up. I honestly don't know how people make it through their teens.

There I go again rambling on and on, forgetting what my whole point to this story is.

So here are the jiffs of what I'm trying to tell you. I was seeing this boy named Taylor Ryans. Well, he wasn't just a boy; he's sixteen going to be seventeen in a month, and has his own car. We were like the most *awesome* couple ever; well, that was until he…well, we'll get to that part later.

Two weeks later, this past Saturday, I saw my so-called best friend Staci hanging all over him after the football game. He ended it with me, which to be honest, I wasn't planning to see him again anyway. He said he didn't need me anymore, that we were finished. But seeing my ex-best friend with him, scared the shit out of me.

Thank God, he doesn't go to the same school as me. I don't know if I could face him after what happened.

I can't stand to look at myself in the mirror.
I'm ugly.
I'm disgusting.

(T)

3 | Skin and Bones

Tuesday

This morning, I roll over in bed and moan because I know that I have gym today. I hate PE; no actually I don't hate gym class, I just hate the fact that we have to get undressed in front of the other girls. Some of us aren't as developed in some areas as others. Me being one of them, but that's not why I hate undressing in front of them.

In the past few days, I haven't eaten much. Okay, okay. I haven't eaten anything in a couple of weeks, since Taylor did what he did. He made a comment that my ass was rounder than most girls my age, and that I should lose some weight. Said I looked hideous and fat.

God, no wonder I hate myself, my life.

I drag myself out of bed, after my mom comes in my room for the third time, and get dressed for school. I have to wait until she leaves the room so she doesn't see what I'm doing to myself. I don't think she'd understand what I'm going through and why I need to do this. I wonder what she'd think of her skank of a daughter. If she only knew what I put myself through.

She didn't seem too concerned when she let me go out with him. Would that make it her fault? No, I did what she asked, and he came over and met with both of my parents. He was a perfect *gentleman.* Of course he was. Otherwise, my parents wouldn't have allowed me to go out with him.

Yeah, like he was a perfect *gentleman* when we were together. If I allow myself to think back to that night a couple weeks ago, it makes me want to vomit.

No wonder I can't eat.

I run to the bathroom and lift the lid of the toilet just as I start to puke.

I know I can't go on like this. I don't want to be reminded of what happened, but I know I will never forget it. Sometimes, I want to reach out to my mom and tell her, but I can't. I know if I do, then everyone in my school will find out. I don't think I could handle the comments they'll say to me—about me. The things they'll call me.

* * *

I flick on the light, trying not to see my reflection in the mirror. I know I'll have to; it's the only way to fix my hair and look presentable. I don't need to give people a reason to ask me what's wrong, although, in the past two weeks I've been good at hiding it.

After using the toilet, I go to my closet and pick out something to wear. I used to be one of those girls that had an outfit laid out the night before, but I'm not that girl anymore.

The way I'm feeling, jogging pants and a huge baggy t-shirt will do. It's like I don't care anymore. Why should I?

My dad takes Rosie to school every day, since he doesn't have to be at work until nine and it's on his way. Her school is in the opposite direction than mine, besides I'd rather just take the bus so I can listen to my music before the noise of the other teenagers filter my day.

I like artists such as Taylor Swift, Adele, One Direction, Vance Joy, and Shawn Mendes, to name a few. They get me out of my head for a while so I don't think about what I'm going to do on Saturday.

The bus pulls up to the school, and we all file out one-by-one like we're robots or something. I have fifteen minutes to get to my locker and then to my class, which is Math. It isn't my favorite class, but I really don't have a favorite. I used to like Art, but it's like I don't care anymore.

* * *

Lunch arrives and Mick is at my locker again waiting to walk with me? I wonder if he knows something's wrong with me. If he can see into my soul and know that I'm dying inside? Just like the way he once felt.

He hasn't said anything. Sometimes at lunch, I catch him looking at me, but I don't say anything. I just go back to reading the book I bring with me. Part of me wants him to ask, to tell him what happened, but what if he tells someone else? Then, it would be all over the school.

I think that's why Layla doesn't talk to him anymore. He's known to take things you say and use them against you, if you give him a reason to.

I remember one time just a couple of months ago when Mick and Layla broke up, and he wasn't too happy about it so he started telling everyone who she was friends with, not to be friends with her because she's a liar and will tear your heart into pieces. Yeah, I guess you could say he didn't take the break-up too well.

That's why I can't talk to anyone. I can't tell anyone what's wrong. Then, the other kids would be looking at me, talking about me, laughing at me. Is that what I think they would do? I don't want to find out, so it's best I just don't say anything to anyone. I'm already lost without Staci. I miss her more than I'm willing to let people know I do. Besides, she's the one who needs to apologize, not me.

It's all my fault.
I can't trust anyone.
I'm ugly.
I'm disgusting.
I don't deserve to live.

(A)

4 | Staci

Wednesday

I see her the moment I step off the bus. It was almost like she wanted to say something to me, but then thought twice about it and walked away. I don't want to think something happened between them. If he did to her, what he did to me. Should I say something to her? Would it help? I would like to know if I'm not the only one.

I close my locker door and turn around almost colliding with Staci, who is now standing right in front of me. There are dark shadows under her eyes, which tells me she hasn't been sleeping and possibly has even stopped eating.

The hall begins to empty, but we don't budge. The first bell rings in the background. I know we need to get to class, but neither one of us moves. Should I say something to her? I want her to speak first since she's the one who started all this between us. As I look at her face, I can tell she isn't mad at me, there's no reason for her to hate me; I didn't go after her ex-boyfriend. Before I can say anything, she whispers, "I'm sorry," and walks away.

* * *

It doesn't take a genius to know that *Taylor strikes again!* Staci doesn't need to tell me; I know by her words. I know by her face, her appearance. No make-up in the world can hide all our faults—our flaws.

I feel like crying, but I can't let anyone see me. I want to go home, but then my mom or dad would have to come get me and I'd have to tell them what's wrong.

That is not an option.

I will myself to move and head to Math class. I walk in the room just as the second bell rings, lucky to have made it at all. Everyone looks at me, but my focus is on Staci who's sitting slouched in her seat near the back of the room. I quickly take my seat before Mrs. Elmer says something to me.

I'm not able to see Staci because my seat happens to be at the front of the class on the other side of the room. You'd think after middle school the teachers would stop assigning seats like we're still babies and let us choose our own seats. I guess I'll have to wait and catch up with her after class if she'll even talk to me, again. I was totally shocked she'd said anything to me to begin with.

The bell rings as I'm trying to get my things organized. When I stand and turn, I don't see her. She must have left already. I quickly run out the door and look around. I know what class she's in next, but mine's in the opposite direction. Now, I'll have to wait until lunch to talk to her.

* * *

The minutes tick slowly by as I continue to check the clock on the wall. It's funny when you're in a hurry time slows down, but when you're not, it's gone and you can't reclaim what you've missed. That's sort of like life. If you don't cherish the moment, they're gone and you can't bring them back, and even if you could alter time, would they even be the same moments you were expecting? Would *you* even be the same person? But that's the thing, isn't it? We will never know because once it's gone—it's forever gone.

By the time lunch arrives, my stomach is in knots. I don't wait for Mick at my locker like every other day, instead I practically run to the cafeteria, looking for Staci. When my eyes find the table she normally sits at, she's not there. I feel defeated and make my way to my table where Mick is waiting for me.

"Where were you a few minutes ago?" he asks.

My mind fumbles for words I don't have. *"Where is Staci?"* is all I have on my mind. I take my seat, but today I didn't bring my book. I don't think I could read it anyway, even if I did have it with me. I have to find Staci. I need to find her. Am I afraid she'll do something stupid? She's not as strong as I am. *Am I strong?* If I was, then why would I be thinking about dying? Too many questions I don't have the answers to.

"Earth to Carly, are you in there?" Mick asks.

I look up and see Alisha staring at me. She has this look of, *"Are you okay?"* on her face.

I blink and focus on Mick's voice. "I'm fine," I say. "I think I might be coming down with something." *Nice save*, I think to myself because the look on both of their faces tells me they believe me, at least I'm hope they do.

I try not to look obvious as my eyes search the cafeteria every few minutes looking for Staci. I'm more positive now that she's left and gone home, unless she's hiding somewhere because of what I think might have happened to her. I hope not because I don't want her to feel the way I do every morning when I wake up—ugly and dirty.

By the end of the day, I'm one-hundred percent sure that she went home because she didn't show up for any of her other classes.

We're ugly.
We're disgusting.
We both feel gross inside.
Do we both want to die.

5 | No Answer
Wednesday Night

After I got home from school, I did nothing but text and call Staci's phone. She always has her phone on her, unlike me who keeps it in my locker until school's out. My parents rule, not mine.

I try to concentrate on my schoolwork, but I can't. I need to know if she's okay. I've known her for a long time and I fear she's not strong enough for what might've happened. Or maybe it's something else. Maybe she just wanted to apologize to me for going out with my ex-boyfriend? We even made a pack not to do something like that to one another. Boys were off-limits when it came to our friendship because we realized it could come between us, and that's what actually happened. We didn't remain friends, and we've been friends since the first grade.

Ugh! I can't stand this anymore. I start pacing in my bedroom, wearing a path in the carpet, when my little sister opens the door. "What are you doing?" she asks.

"What does it look like?" I bark at her. Her face starts to crumble and tears instantly appear. "I'm sorry, Rosie. I didn't mean to yell at you." I walk over to her and open my arms, but now she's mad at me and runs away, slamming her bedroom door. "Great," I mumble, knowing she will tell mom and dad when they get home. I turn, slam my door, and fall onto my bed, facedown.

Shit, shit, shit.

* * *

The minute my mom knocks on my bedroom door, I know that Rosie has told her what I did.

"Can I come in?" my mom asks.

"Yeah," I reply. Like what could I actually say other than yes? *"No, you can't come in;"* yeah, like that'd go over well with her—with both my parents. I'd be grounded until the end of my freshman year.

She opens the door enough to slip in and then closes it behind her. She walks over to the bed and sits down beside me as I pretend to do my homework.

"What seems to be the problem?" she asks.

Before I let her say another word, my mouth jumbles out the words I didn't want her to know. "Mom, I'm sorry for taking it out on Rosie; it's just that Staci and I aren't…" I stop speaking. She doesn't know about Staci and me not being friends anymore because I haven't even told her that Taylor and I aren't dating anymore either. I have to think of something because if I know my mom, she'll start asking questions and giving me the third-degree like I'm her client. Someone she's defending, and I can't tell her what happened. Not yet.

I can tell by the look on her face that she's about to start interrogating me, but I talk first. "Staci and I had a fight; that's all, Mom. I'm sorry for yelling at Rosie. I just had a bad day, that's all," I say in my most sympathetic voice.

She takes a long look at me before saying, "Okay, but you need to go apologize to your little sister."

That was way too easy.

Talk To Me

She hugs me and then I feel her freeze in our embrace. She knows. She can feel how thin I am. She releases me and takes my chin in her hand, looking into my eyes as if she can see my soul or read my thoughts. "Are you sure everything's okay with you?"

I nod, hoping she'll believe me and leave because if I was to speak right now, I think I might start crying.

She kisses my forehead, "Just so you know, you can always talk to me; I was once a teenager too. I might be able to help," she says and smiles before leaving the room.

My body collapses against the headboard. "Thank God," I mumble. I thought for sure she'd try and get what is bothering me, out of me, but I just can't tell her.

After I finish my homework, I knock on my little sister's door before opening it and sticking my head inside. She's sitting on the floor at the end of her bed, playing with her Barbies. I sit down beside her, grab a doll she's not playing with and start smoothing down its hair and fixing the clothes. Why does that seem to be the first thing we girls do when we're playing with dolls?

Neither one of us says anything; we just sit in the quiet room. This seems to make me stop and think that I don't know if I can go through with ending my life on Saturday. I look at my sister without moving my head. My eyes watch as she fiddles with the dress she's trying to put on her Barbie.

I'll miss this.

I'll miss her.

I don't know if I can just disappear.

To think only of myself, and not her or the rest of my family.

It seems selfish, and now I feel ashamed for even thinking I could just swallow a whole bunch of pills and be done with this world.

Be done with Rosie.

A single tear leaks from my eye and rolls down my cheek. I think Rosie notices because now she's hugging me and saying she's sorry, even though she's not the one who needs to apologize.

I am.

I wrap my arms around her and tell her I'm sorry for yelling at her, and now we're both crying and laughing.

There's a knock on the door. Dad sticks his head in to tell us it's time to eat. Normally, I can get away with not eating by using my homework as an excuse, but I've finished all of it and to be honest, I'm starving.

Rosie is the first one on her feet and then me. I watch her take off down the hall, and I think about how much I love my little sister and that I still should go through with my first plan. I still have to end my life because she doesn't deserve to have a sister like me.

She deserves someone so much better. Someone she can look up to, and I'm not that person.

* * *

I'm alone in my room, but that only happens after Rosie goes to bed. Because of what happened earlier, she was attached to my side.

I sit beneath my blankets with my laptop perched on my lap. I search the web about what I should do. I don't find anything different than what I've read the past couple of weeks.

-Avoid secluded places. (We were in the school parking lot.)

-Don't spend time alone with people that make you feel uncomfortable. (I felt very comfortable with him. That's the problem.)

- Stay sober. (I wasn't drinking.)

- Be clear on the relationship you want with the person. (It honestly never crossed my mind.)

- Don't let peer pressure push you into doing something you don't want to do. (He was the only one pressuring me.)

- Take self-defense courses. (Too late for that.)

All these precautions are great to know, but in my circumstances, a little too late. I click on another link and it takes me to what you should do afterwards.

- Go straight to the emergency room. (Then my parents would know.)

- Call or text someone you feel safe with. (That's the thing; I did feel safe with him.)

- If you aren't sure what to do, call a crisis center. (I had wanted to do it weeks ago, but each time I went to dial the number, I hung up the phone. Would it even matter now? It's not like it happened yesterday. What would they tell me? Would they say it's my fault? That I should have known it would happen with someone much older than me? I don't know if I could handle the person on the phone blaming me.)

I read further down the page and it lists things that you should do even if it did happen days or weeks ago. It says it's not just physically damaging—it can be emotionally traumatic as well.

No shit, Sherlock!

It may be hard to talk or think about what happened, but talking with a health professional can help in the healing process. Then, I wonder if I should and if they'd tell my parents. Something I'm not quite ready to do.

I'm ugly.
I'm disgusting.
I should drink a bottle of bleach.

(L)

6 | Staci
Thursday

Morning comes way too soon. I don't want to get out of bed. The blankets are warm and I snuggle into them, knowing the knock on my door will be arriving soon to get me up for school.

The only positive thing will be to see Staci. I'll wait by her locker this time so we can talk before class. I know I didn't see her yesterday, but I'm hoping she comes to school today. Maybe I should send her a text?

I reach for my phone, but it's dead because I forgot to put it on the charger last night. I grab the cord beside my bed and plug it in. It only needs a minute or two and then I can turn it on. When I do, there's a message from Staci. I click on the icon and listen to the voicemail that she had left last night around 1:00 a.m.

> ***"Hi Carly, I just wanted to hear your voice one last time, but I know from calling that your phone is shut off or you forgot to charge it again. So…"*** she pauses.
>
> ***"So I'm going to just tell you that I'm sorry. I'm sorry for ruining our friendship over a boy. I'm sorry I didn't come talk to you about the way I feel before I let the issues eat me up alive. I'm sorry I wasn't a good enough friend***

> ***to you like you were to me. But…"*** she pauses again, crying harder and sniffling in the receiver.
>
> ***"But I wonder if he did to you what he did to me? Did he hurt you too? Did he take a piece of you that held you together? Did you or do you think of what life will be like now? I do and I can't face it. I'm sorry, but I can't… I can't feel anything—anymore. Please forgive me, Carly; I'm so sorry for everything."*** She whispers two more words that I barely hear. ***"Help Jessica."***

The line goes dead.

The message is over.

"Help Jessica," replays in my head. Jessica who? Who the hell is Jessica?

I hit the play button again and listen to the message, hanging onto every word. Once it ends, I hit the call button and listen as it rings. After the third ring, someone picks up, but it's not Staci. It's Staci's mom, Mrs. Garrison.

"Hello…" she whispers, "Carly, are you there? I know it's you. I saw your name on the caller ID."

"Yes, Mrs. G, I'm here." I've been calling her Mrs. G since Staci and I first met because it was so much easier. I hear her sniffle, wanting to ask, but I don't because in my heart I already know.

"Carly, I'm so sorry I have to tell you this over the phone, but..." she sniffles again. "Staci... Staci hung herself last night," she bawls into the phone.

"Staci killed herself?" I repeat into the phone.

"Yes," Mrs. Garrison replies.

My mouth drops open. I'm speechless.

I don't know what to say, so I don't say anything. I don't even wait for Mrs. G to say anything else. I just let my cell phone fall from my hand and hit the floor with a thud.

My best friend in the whole world killed herself. Staci did what I wanted to do all along, but she beat me to it. I'll never see my best friend again. I'll never see Staci at my locker. I'll never laugh with her again. I'll never have her over for a sleepover. We won't go to the same college. We won't get to do anything ever again!

The tears come on fast and hard as I start repeating the same words over and over again into the room. The words get louder and louder each time I say them. My mom opens the door, followed by my dad. I keep yelling what I won't get to do with Staci. My mom sits down beside me on the bed. I turn to her, my face red and puffy from crying and screaming.

"I can't do this anymore!" I scream at my mom's face. "I can't hide my hurt anymore." I start to rock back and forth. My mom grabs ahold of me, wrapping her arms around me. I can hear my mom shushing me, but she doesn't know what I know, does she? There's no way my mom knows!

My mom pulls away and looks at me. I can't tell if she's heard what happened to my best friend. I can't believe Staci took her own life from what he did to her, what he did to us, but isn't that what I was going to do? Wasn't I going to let Taylor win? How is that fair? *Two can keep a secret if one of them is dead.*

I suck in a breath. I don't have to let him win. I can tell my parents right now, and the world would know because I know that my mother would get justice for what he's done. But I can't open my mouth and tell my mom what happened.

My mom must see the phone on the floor because she bends over and picks it up and places it to her ear.

"Hello," my mom says.

A few seconds later, my mom's hand flies to her mouth and she starts to cry and says that she's so sorry for Mrs. Garrison's loss. My mom sets the phone face down on my nightstand, and then looks at me as she's wiping the tears away. "I'm so sorry, sweetheart," my mom says, giving me another hug.

I can feel her embrace; it's strangling me. I feel like I can't breathe. I need her to let go so I can breathe. I suck in air, and then another; before I know it, I'm hyperventilating. My mom lets go of me and touches my face, telling me to slow down and take short breaths. Once my breathing gets back to normal, I lie my head down on the pillow.

"You're staying home from school today," my mom says.

I nod and turn to my side. I want my parents to leave the room so I can be left alone. I just want to be alone. I need to think about what I should do or shouldn't do. I don't know anymore. Right now, I feel like dying. My insides are already dying and I can't stop it. I can't think of anything but Staci and what Taylor did to her, to us.

I think that if I would've talked to Staci yesterday. If I would've had my phone charged and heard my best friend calling, would I have saved her? Now that's something I'll have to live with for the rest of my life. Saturday's only two days away, but I don't know if I can go through with it now.

My parents finally leave the room, and I'm left with my mind twirling. Every thought you could possibly imagine is floating through my head. I can't stop them from entering.

"I'm sorry, Staci," I say into my pillow as the tears cascade down my face. "I'm so so sorry." The tears won't stop. I can't stop them from falling.

My mom comes back into the room and hands me a pill with a glass of water. I recognize the shape; it's one of her Xanax. I quickly swallow it down and hand her back the glass. She sets it down on the nightstand and leaves the room. Before I know what hits me, I feel drowsy and sleep takes me away from the living, and I feel at peace.

I miss Staci.
I'm so sorry for what I didn't do.
I'm ugly.
I'm disgusting.
I deserve to die.

(O)

7 | Too Late

Still Thursday

When I finally wake from slumber, my eyes feel swollen and crusted at the corners from crying so much. When I start to sit up, my head feels dizzy, and that was only from taking one pill, but I also haven't had anything to eat since dinner last night.

I throw my legs off the bed and stand, using the nightstand as stability. At least I know now what one pill will do to me—I can just imagine five or ten. So, I know it will work, and I wouldn't hurt anymore. My heart wouldn't ache from missing Staci. If I would have said something, anything, she'd still be here with me, and we'd be hanging out, talking like old times.

"You should do it," the voice whispers in my head. "Where in the hell did that come from?" I mumble.

I shake the thoughts from my head and walk to the bathroom. I use the toilet, flush, and step in front of the mirror. It's the first time in a long while that I actually stand here looking at myself in the mirror. I mean *really* looking at myself. I can't believe how skinny I am, and my hair is starting to thin and look scraggly.

I really do look hideous and ugly.

Taylor was right.

No one would want me now. I'm just a washed-up *hoe* who lost her best friend. No, I'm a washed-up, ugly *hoe* that no one will ever want again. I don't deserve to live in this world with all the other beautiful people.

"Screw this," I say to the girl in the mirror as I slam the side of my fist on the marble counter. I head to my closet to get my stash of pills from my secret box without even thinking twice or letting my mind try to change the decision I've just made.

I set the box down on my nightstand, open it, and take out the pills. I dump a handful of pills in the palm of my hand and toss them in my mouth, while gulping down the glass of water my mom left on the nightstand for me. I can taste the grittiness as one of the pills gets stuck at the back of my throat. I drink more water until it goes down my throat.

I look down to see how many I have left—five. Should I save them or take them? Well, if it doesn't work this time, I can always try it again. *Screw it*, I toss them in my mouth and one hits the side of my mouth and falls to the floor, but I don't care; these will have to do the job. What I've taken will have to be enough to kill me. They just have to *be!*

"It didn't take that long for the first pill to work," I think to myself. If I'm going to leave a note, I should write one now before it's too late. I should say goodbye to my baby sister and even my big sister Kyra who I'll miss the most. We have always been close sisters and shared things with one another. I should also tell my mom and dad how much I love them because it's not something this family says a lot. We don't share words of love.

I walk over to the desk along the wall and sit down. There's a tray of loose-leaf paper; I grab one sheet and start to write. I almost start to write about Taylor, but I don't want him to be in my goodbye letter. Just the thought of his name makes me nauseous.

I finish with "I love all of you, and I'm sorry it had to come to this, but I didn't know any other way to deal with what happened to me." I write my name at the bottom of the page and lay the pen down beside the note.

I stand to go lie down in my bed, and my legs feel like they're about to buckle under my weight. My stomach spasms and I think I'm going to throw-up. By the time I reach the bathroom, I don't have time to open the lid of the toilet and vomit goes everywhere. I fall to my knees and hang my head over the tub.

I don't hear my mom come into the room when I heave one more time. How can there be anything in me? I didn't eat more than a few bites of food last night.

"Oh, my God, Carly, what's wrong?" my mom shouts before she kneels down beside me, moving my long brown hair away from my face. She then yells for my dad, saying that something is wrong and that I need to go to the hospital.

My mom helps me sit back on my heels, and then cradles me in her arms. My dad appears, looking frantic, then bolts out of the room. I can vaguely hear him on the phone as the room starts to go fuzzy. Did the pills have enough time to get through my system? Seems unlikely to me, but I don't feel good at all.

I hear the muffled voice of my dad talking so he must be in my room. *"Shit the note!"* I think to myself before everything goes black…

I'm worthless.
I'm pathetic.
I can't even kill myself.
I'm ugly.
I'm disgusting.
Please don't save me.

(R)

8 | Questions

Friday

When I open my eyes, I can see my mom sitting in a chair next to me, reading a book. I'm not sure how long I've been out, or where I am because the room doesn't look like the same room my grandpa was in last year when he was in the hospital.

I look at my mom the same time she looks at me. She smiles and sets her book down on the table next to the bed.

"How are you feeling?" she asks.

"Okay, I guess," I say back. *Not dead,* I think to myself.

"Your dad was here earlier, but hospital policy is only one guest at a time."

I give her a smile so she knows that I understand. Should I ask her where I am? Actually, I think I know. I'm sure they saw the note on my desk. Now, I'm just waiting for my mom to ask me to say something. The words she says next come out almost like a whisper, but I hear them.

"Why, Carly? Please, talk to me."

I turn to face her, but I just can't tell her why. I'm not ready to share my secret with her. Tears stream down my face; I turn and look the other way. I can't talk to her now. I'm so confused on what to do. Keeping the secret will destroy me, but so will telling it. I don't want my parents to think less of me. I don't want them to say that I deserved it and that I am ugly, disgusting, and hideous. I don't think I could live with them thinking those things about me. That their daughter was so stupid and careless.

My mom touches my hand and gives it a squeeze. "I love you no matter what," she says. "Please, just talk to me. I can't help you if you don't open up to me. I won't judge you or love you any less. Please, Carly, talk to me."

The last part hits me hard and uncontrollable tears blur everything before my eyes. I squeeze them shut, trying to close out her voice too. I don't want to hear what she has to say. It will only hurt me more. Like I haven't hurt myself enough already.

I slide my hand out of hers and turn my body to face the opposite wall. My mom and I have never been that close. She was always too busy working to care about me. Besides, I can take care of myself.

Inside, I laugh at this thought. If it's true that I really am strong enough to take care of myself, then how did I end up here, still alive, in a place where everything I have left of myself will be taken from me? I may be stupid when it comes to boys, but I'm not a fool. I'm sure they've locked me up in some nuthouse with other people just like me.

I was once the baby of the family, but Rosie took that away from me. Not that I want to be the baby anymore, and I can't blame her—she's innocent in all of this, and too young to understand anyway.

I cry harder.

Talk To Me

My mom stands up and leaves the room. I hear the door click shut behind her. Now it's just me and my thoughts.

Not a good combination, considering how I got here.

I'm ugly.
I'm disgusting.
I'm skinny.
I deserve so much worse.

(R)

9 | Doctors' Orders

Now I'm stuck in the place that I was stupid enough to get myself put in, but how did I know what my body would do when I took the pills? I thought I'd just fall asleep and not wake up, like the first pill my mom gave me. Instead, I was a vomiting mess. My body was rejecting the pills; at least that's what the doctors have told me. Doctors plural because I have like three of them now.

The first doctor checks my fluid intake because I was starving myself to death. I'm on an IV because I refuse to eat. I guess she's more of a nutritional consultant. She also monitors my food intake; although, I think I'm making her job easy because I'm not giving her anything to monitor.

The second doctor checks my test results. Blood work, CT scans, etc. Everything that I had to have done when I arrived here. The tests I assume show what's going on inside my body.

The third doctor tries to get me to talk about whatever's going on inside me, except I don't want to talk to him about what's bothering me. He doesn't think I know what a psychiatrist does. He keeps reminding me that whatever I say will be held in strictest confidence. That I won't need to worry about anyone finding out about what we discuss, what we talk about. He says that talking will help me feel better. Will help me heal and not want to die. Part of me knows he's right. It's just like what I read on all those sites. Talking is the first step.

But am I ready?

* * *

I'm in a place they call *One Stepp Closer*; which my mom says will help me. It's a place where juvenile kids go when they try to kill themselves or have a tough time socializing with others, meaning they act-out in ways that we teenagers shouldn't. It's almost like we do these things for attention, but I can swear to you that I was not trying to get my parents' attention. I would've done that by just telling them what happened to me.

These facilities are where we teenagers can feel better and get the help we are told we need. I know she's right, but it still doesn't make me feel any better. It doesn't erase what happened to Staci and me.

It's only been one-and-a-half days, but it feels like forever, and I'm finally allowed to get out of bed and walk around. You really don't know how much you miss doing something until you're told that you can't do it anymore or at least, not for a while.

The only catch is that I have to bring the IV stand with me. Otherwise, I will be strapped to a bed, and I don't think I could handle that. These past two days have been a struggle for me, not being able to get out of bed and move around.

I exit my room and walk down the long hallway. The walls are painted a crème color with posters hanging on them. They're all different, but they all mean the same thing. They are slogans to help you feel better, like a cat hanging from a rope, ‘Hang in there’; another one says, ‘One Day at a Time’.

I can hear people talking and laughing as I make my way further down the hall. I stop at a room that’s three times as big as the one they’re keeping me in.

I see several kids that are about my age. Some are playing cards, some are just sitting by a TV talking and joking around, and there’s a couple playing ping-pong. I haven’t seen that game in a long time, but I was pretty good at it when we had a ping-pong table in our basement years ago. Then it hits me that Staci and I were the ones who played ping-pong together. My stomach tightens at the memory.

I start to back out of the doorway when a girl from across the room spots me, which stops me in my tracks.

She walks over, “You don’t have to leave. We’ve all been waiting for you to be allowed out of your room.” Everyone turns as she says this to me.

Part of me wants to turn and walk very fast back to my room because honestly if I run, I’d probably hurt myself. I take one step backwards, but she’s in front of me before I’m even out the door.

“Don’t leave, we won’t bite,” she smiles.

Next thing I know, everyone in the room is joining her at the door. Well, all except for two girls at the back of the room who seem to be watching me.

I can feel my back tense-up, and I grip the IV pole that I’m holding in my left hand. I swallow and look at all their faces. Some of them look older than me, and I wonder what they’re in here for. Did they try to kill themselves too? Are we all suicidal and have to be locked up together?

Before I can speak, someone grabs my free hand and lures me into the room towards the sofa.

"Hi, my name's Jordan, and this is Scott, Mike, Adriana, Marci, Jake, Becki, and Gabby," she says as she points a finger at each one when she says their names.

"Hi," I say back, my throat sounding hoarse. I don't really care about these people because I don't plan to stay here long enough to get to know them. I don't belong here anyway.

The one named Gabby says, "So why are you in here? Did you try to starve yourself to death? I only ask because you are almost as skinny as the kids in Africa."

"Gab, why do you have to say it like that? You'll scare the girl and then she won't talk," Jordan replies. "Now you know why her name is Gabby; she likes to gab a lot." Everyone laughs; even Gabby joins in.

"I just don't like to eat." That's all I say because I'm not going to tell them the real reason I stopped eating.

"Once you start eating, they'll take that IV out of your arm," Jake says.

Between him and Scott, he's the better looking one. "*What was that?*" I scold myself. *I'm still alive and allowed to look,* I think to myself. The kid Mike seems shy, and he's sort of standing near the back of the group so he's not noticed as much.

I think Jordan's the head of the group because she seems to be the outspoken one. The other two girls,

Gabby and Becki, seem to agree with whatever Jordan says.

I look around at all of them as if they're waiting for the Pope to speak. I'm no Pope, so they better skedaddle away from me and go back to doing whatever they were doing before I came along.

I sit down near the arm of the chair, and the girl I think whose name is Becki sits down next to me. Her hair is the same color as mine, brown but with natural loose curls that spray out of her messy bun. "Don't worry about Gabby, we all have our reasons for being here," Becki states. "Besides we all have group together so you'll learn more about all of us soon enough. Mike here has been in this place the longest. He used to be a cutter. Marci here," she points her thumb to the redhead standing near the back wall next to another girl who's wearing all black, possibly Goth, "Would burn herself with cigarettes to feel the pain and forget about what hurt her in the first place, and I'm in here because I tried to off myself by asphyxiation." She shows me the marks on her neck from whatever she used to try and kill herself.

I suck in a breath because it makes me think of Staci, and I honestly don't want to know what Becki went through, but she continues talking.

"My little brother walked in and saved my life so my parents brought me here. Adriana arrived here two weeks ago; so she's the newest besides you."

I can feel my mouth fall open, but then close it before one of them notices. They don't need to know the real reason I'm here. If they want to think it's because I starve myself, then let them.

Jordan says that we meet for group every day at 1:00 p.m., and sometimes in the evening around seven, depending on the counselor. I nod and before I know it, my nurse beckons me back to my room. Everyone, but the two girls by the wall named Adriana and Marci, says goodbye. Becki says she'll see me later as we go our separate ways.

I'm ugly.
I'm skinny.
I don't want to be here.

10 | Therapy

I can't believe that Saturday flew by—the day I was supposed to take my own life—and now it's Sunday. I wake up drenched in my own sweat. It wouldn't be the first time I've had a nightmare, and I'm sure it won't be the last. I was just thankful my mom wasn't here. She would've asked a bunch of questions. *"What was the dream about?"—I'm not telling you. "Do you want to talk about what's bothering you?"—No. "How often do you have them?"—Every damn night since it happened. God, Mom, just leave me alone...* but she isn't here. It's just my thoughts torturing me to death; I guess that's another way to end my pitiful life.

You'd think she was my psychiatrist and not a lawyer. She always has a lot of questions. I guess that falls in-line with being an attorney. They're made for questioning and badgering the witness. But I'm not a witness; I'm a victim.

* * *

Visiting hours start at 11:00 a.m. and end at 2:00 p.m., mine just ended twenty minutes ago. It was nice seeing Rosie again, even though it has only been two days since I saw her last. She looked sad, although I can't blame her—I tried to kill myself and she doesn't understand why. *I wonder how my parents have explained it to her? I wonder if they even told my sister Kyra what happened to me? They probably don't want to disrupt her schooling. To them, school and studying is more important than family, at least that's what I feel.*

Hell, sometimes I don't understand the things I do, either, or the way my mind works. I'm scared and don't know what to do. Most of the time, I feel alone and empty.

I thought if I just ended my life, I would go to a better place, but for whom? I would be dead and my family would be the ones suffering over it. Would that justify what happened to me…to us—Staci and me? Now that Staci is gone, did it make her life, as short as it was, more meaningful? How does that solve our problems and what happened to us?

My mom told me before they left that Staci's parents will be having the funeral on Wednesday. She said that she'd bring a dress for me and that we'd all go together. I'm not sure if I want to go. Will the casket be open or closed? Will I be able to keep it together or fall apart? If I lose-it everyone will be looking at me, and I don't need that kind of attention.

Now that things have quieted down a little bit after visiting hours, I decide to walk out in the hallway again, staying away from the room where everyone else goes. I want to be alone with my worries and questions, and moving around helps me to think.

* * *

In the past few weeks before Staci and I stopped talking, we swore that no one would come between us and that we would stay friends until the end of time. At the end of a call or text, at the end of every day, we would always say, "*Don't ever leave me*", but she left, didn't she?

By the time I get back to my room, I feel like I need a nap. I'm so exhausted dragging this IV thing around with me. I wish they would just take it out, but I know they won't unless I give them something back in return.

I need to eat.

The sad part is, before the last couple of weeks happened, I loved food. I ate every day, and I wasn't like fat or anything; I just wasn't as skinny as I am now.

I wonder what they'd do if I took the needle out of my arm. Would an alarm sound if I did? Would they strap me to the bed? It's funny how things enter your mind that you don't normally think about.

Becki enters my room about ten minutes after I do, and sits down in the chair against the wall. She's the last person I wanted to see after just thinking about Staci's death, hanging herself.

"You ready for therapy today? You can walk with me if you want to," she says.

I nod, "Okay." *Well, I guess if I have to go to this, it's best I go with someone who knows what's going on,* I admit to myself.

I must look nervous because Becki says, "Don't be scared. Once you go to the first meeting it will get easier," she smiles.

It's not really about going to the meeting. It's the fact that I don't want to talk about what happened to me with some people I don't know. Do they really think they can help me get past this? All by opening up and telling them about my best friend Staci? I can't even talk to my mom and dad, who would actually be the first people I might tell, not some kids I've never met. Some strangers.

I was so thankful my mom brought some clothes from home. They said I could wear jogging pants and sweatshirts if I wanted to. So, that's what I had her bring me. My dad wasn't very talkative when they were here. I think he's afraid of what I might do. What I tried to do to myself.

I guess I didn't really think about how my family would feel after I was gone. I wonder if any of these thoughts crossed Staci's mind before she took her final leap.

I didn't think about what it would do to them; I only thought about ending my pain. I guess that makes me selfish, but that's usually how most teenagers are. We don't think of how others will feel; we only think about the here and now and what it's doing to us. In our minds, the world is small and everything needs to be our own way. Although, I shouldn't speak for everyone my age, not every teenager is selfish and closed-minded. Not everyone wants to die.

I tell Becki to give me a minute while I have the nurse help me change my clothes. I have trouble with the IV being in the way. I was hoping she'd remove it, but no way. Once I'm done, we walk side-by-side to therapy.

* * *

The meeting room is the same size as the activity room, though I refer to it as our sanctuary, our home away from home. That's the room with the TV and ping-pong table, which I have yet to play.

There's at least ten chairs sitting in a circle, and I actually take the time to count all of them in my head. One must be for the therapist because there are only nine of us.

This is the first time I'm actually participating in therapy because the nurse allowed me to miss Saturday's session due to being stressed-out. At least, that's what I made her think.

Becki takes her seat first, and then I sit next to her. In the couple of days that I've been here, Becki is the nicest, and so is Jordan. I've noticed that Adriana and Marci seem to be more aggressive. Okay, they're little bitches.

The moment they walk in the room and see me sitting next to Becki, Marci comes over and tells me to find another seat because I'm in her chair. That's funny because I don't remember seeing her name on it.

I stand and take the chair on the other side of Becki before Gabby comes in the room. Gabby sits down next to me and smiles. She starts talking to me, but then stops when she sees Ms. Thompson come in the room. There must be a *no-talking* policy, but then that wouldn't make sense because it's a therapy group; we're supposed to talk.

Ms. Thompson introduces me to the group, even though I'd already met them yesterday, but she wouldn't know that. Then she asks who wants to talk first, but no one takes the bait.

"Mike, do you have anything you want to share today?" she smiles at him.

He shrugs his shoulders. I'd noticed yesterday how shy he can be, if he wants to. He's also the one that's been here the longest, according to Becki. Maybe it's because I'm the new girl and he doesn't want me to get the wrong impression about him.

Ms. Thompson moves on to Scott who summarizes his past week at this facility; and then how he ended up in *One Stepp Closer*. Scott's sixteen years old and was found with a gun in his room. His parents found out that he had taken the gun from his uncle's house, who's a police officer, and was planning on killing himself after he was wasted on heroin, which he had bought off some druggie in Joliet. Scott's choices were Juvenile lock-up for stealing the gun or here. It doesn't take a genius to choose to come here over jail.

Next, it's Marci's turn to talk. She's fifteen and used to burn herself with cigarettes. Her father molested her every other day when he was either drunk or high on cocaine. Her aunt brought her here after she discovered what was going on.

After everyone who wanted to share their story talked, they all looked over at me. I wasn't ready to tell anyone why I was here. I didn't even know these people, even if they were comfortable telling me their problems. I wasn't that eager to be called names. Or even have people feel sorry for me.

I'm ugly.
I'm hideous.
I don't need to be here.
I want to go home.

(A)

11 | Funeral

The next couple of days slipped away and before I know it, it's Wednesday. My mom said she'd be here early, sometime around nine in the morning because the services started at ten with the funeral following afterwards.

I didn't sleep much last night so I'm trying to cover my tired, swollen eyes with some make-up Jordan gave me. I still don't want to go. I was up all night crying and since I haven't been eating; I'm fragile and weak.

They, meaning the doctors, took out my IV this morning, but told me I'd have a new one when I get back later today. My mom said we could go back to our house for a little bit before I have to come back here. I guess so I can grab some more of my things if I want to.

I wish we were allowed to have our cell phones, but it's not like anyone will be texting me. So why should I care?

* * *

I feel sick to my stomach as we approach the building where the service is being held. My dad parks and we all get out of the car. My mom holds onto my arm like I need help standing up. Maybe I do and just don't know it; come to think of it, my legs do feel heavy as if they're encased in cement. Rosie grabs ahold of my other arm, but her touch feels good.

Once we're inside the memorial building, the first thing my eyes see is the casket. Not Staci's mom or dad, who are crying and hugging people, but the casket with my best friend inside. The casket is open, but I don't know if I can walk up there and see her—my stomach tightens.

I've been to other funerals before, but this one seems different because we were closer than I was with my Grandpa Randy who died last year from lung cancer.

We get in line for our turn to say our regrets to Staci's parents, but I know I'll fall to pieces when I look at Mrs. G. She was—no, *is*—like a second mom to me, and this will be hard. I can hear her all the way down the line.

We didn't show up late, but there are still a lot of people in front of us. I feel bad for Mrs. G because Staci was her only child. She doesn't get to love another kid. She won't get to see her daughter go to prom or even help her on her wedding day, like so many other moms get to do.

Again, I think about what I did to myself. I wonder if Mrs. Garrison knows that I took a handful of pills later that day. Would she scold me like I was a bad kid? Would she look down upon me and think I was being like Staci? Don't they know how much we loved each other? We were more than just friends; we were like sisters.

I look around the room to help pass the time, and I freeze when I see him standing there talking to the members of the football team. I wonder why he's here. He doesn't deserve to say goodbye to her. Doesn't he know that it's his fault she killed herself?

A shiver courses up my spine and I think my mom felt it too because she looks over at me and follows my eyes. Does she know that we're not together anymore?

She must know something because she says," Honey, are you feeling all right? Do you want to sit down? You're as white as a ghost, Carly."

I feel my legs start to go out from under me, and my dad quickly slips his arms around me to hold me up. "I think we should sit down. Maybe this is too much for you, too soon," my dad says.

I shake my head because I don't want to cause a scene. I don't want *him* to come over and start talking to me. I have to get a grip.

Once we get through the line and see Staci, then we can just go home. We don't have to stay, but I know that my parents will insist that we do. My mom will make me feel bad and remind me that Staci was my best friend and that it would be wrong to just walk out, but don't they know how hard this is for me. That I don't think I can say goodbye to my best friend whom I haven't spoken to in two weeks.

The line moves forward and we're two people away from Mrs. and Mr. G. I swallow because I don't know if I can do this. It's taking everything inside me to just stand here and act like everything's okay, but I know once I'm face-to-face with Mrs. G, I'll fall completely apart.

My breathing starts to speed up, and I know I'm about to start hyperventilating in front of all these people, but I don't know how to stop.

Next thing I know, my mom is speaking to Mrs. Garrison. She's saying how sorry she is for her loss, and that if she needs anything, anything at all, to just ask.

My dad gently pushes me forward; I look up and meet first Mr. Garrison's eyes and then Mrs. Garrison. Tears leak from my eyes the moment I see her, and I become a total mess. The sobs come slow at first, but then I'm hugging myself so tight, I can't move.

I feel arms circling my shoulders, gripping them so I don't fall to the floor. My mom and dad help me out of line and we go outside where I can get some fresh air.

Rosie is clenched to my leg, sobbing along with me. I want to comfort her, but I don't know how. I can't even take care of me.

Once I get ahold of myself, I gaze past my parents and see all of my classmates. I see Mick standing with Alisha; they're whispering to each other, but I don't think it's as bad as I'm imagining it is—that they're talking about me; judging me—but what do I know?

All eyes are now on me, and I feel like running away. They're all gawking at me and probably whispering about how Staci and me so deserved what happened to us, that we were stupid to allow it to happen. Do they know what happened? Did Staci tell anyone?

"Carly, do you want to stay? Or should we just leave?" I hear my mom ask.

My mind is spinning; I don't know what I want. Is it wrong for me not to say goodbye to the only best friend I've ever had? Should I just walk back in there and face

Staci head-on. Stare down at her cold, hard body and tell her that I'm so sorry for what happened to her? Will my legs let me walk in there and past all the people that don't really care about her the way I did—*I do.*

"Carly, can you hear me?" my mom asks again.

I nod as everything around me gets loud, then I feel her hand touch my face and turn me towards her. "Can you hear me? Do you want to stay?"

"I… I don't know," I whisper.

I look down where Rosie is; my dad has knelt down to her level and is holding her tight. I can't help but feel responsible for doing this to her. If I hadn't freaked out, would she be clinging to my leg, afraid of me doing something to myself again?

My head starts to hurt from all the thinking that I'm doing and I want to sit down. I want to… I still don't know what I want to do.

* * *

I'm not sure what time it is, but when I lift my head from my mom's shoulder the line that was once there has disappeared.

"I think it's time for the service to begin," my mom whispers in my ear.

I stand, knowing I'll regret this if I don't at least stay for the services before Staci is placed in the ground where I will never see her again. "Let's go in," I say.

Rosie takes my hand and we walk together into the building. The room is full of people from one wall to the other. In front, stands Mr. G at a podium. He's speaking about how wonderful a person Staci was and I tense up.

I don't think I can hear this. I feel like I'm the worst friend to her because I can't even listen to her family's speech. Then I hear my name, and everyone turns and looks right at me. I go stiff and feel Rosie tug on my arm.

"Can I go with you?" she asks.

But I don't know where she thinks I'm going. Then I hear Mr. Garrison say my name again. "Carly would you like to say a few words? You and Staci were like sisters. You were so close."

Not as close as you think. I blink, and Rosie and I walk up the middle row to where Mr. G is standing. I hear Mrs. Garrison next to me sniffling and blowing her nose in a Kleenex. I take in a deep breath and stand next to Staci's father. I hadn't noticed earlier that he had shaved off his beard, but I also haven't seen him in two weeks, going on three.

He holds out his hand and I take it. He squeezes gently before moving back from the podium and I move forward, Rosie stuck to my side.

I look up, the faces of the kids I go to school with stare back at me, waiting for me to speak. I swallow and let the words leave my throat and whisper through the air.

> *"Staci was my best friend. We met in the first grade after moving here from St. Louis. She was the first person to sit next to me at the lunch table and since that day, we were inseparable,"* I say as tears start to fall. *"She was*

like a sister to me who always wanted to hang out and copied me in everything I did," I smile at this. *"Sometimes I thought it was irritating, but I came to love her more than anything. She was my anchor that kept me from drowning. We..."* I paused. *"We did everything together and I will miss her. No, I miss her so much now and wish she was here."* Tears cascade down my face. I wipe them away. *"She didn't need to die. She shouldn't have died, and I blame only one person for her death."*

The place went silent and I knew I had two choices. One, I could tell them what happened or two, stop talking and walk away. I will have some explaining to do later as I see the look on my parents' faces from the words I just spoke, and as much as I'd like to look Taylor straight in the eyes, I don't because this isn't the time or place. This day is for Staci; I don't dare give him the satisfaction.

I squeeze Rosie's hand and step back from the podium. I walk over to the casket that holds my best friend and whisper close to her ear, "He will pay for what he's done to us." That's when I remember the last words she said last, "Help Jessica."

I'm still fragile.
But…
I'm getting stronger.

(N)

12 | No Goodbye

After the services, we climb in the car and follow everyone to the cemetery where Staci will be laid to rest for all eternity. The whole way there, I could feel my dad's eyes on me through the rearview mirror. I knew after this was over, there would be a talk. I still felt sad for the loss of my best friend, but somehow I also felt stronger.

Of course, I had no intentions on saying what I did. I wasn't planning on speaking at her funeral—period! I was in a mental hospital or at least, that's what I call it for trying to kill myself, but now I felt I had a job to do.

Staci didn't have to die. She shouldn't have ended her life because of some boy. Though I haven't room to talk, I was thinking the same thing. I was going to allow the same boy to win, but I can't do that. I need to help my friend Staci by helping Jessica, but… I don't know who this Jessica girl is. Then it came to me, I'll have to go to a football game and find her. I shiver and my stomach flips just thinking about it. I haven't been to a football game since I saw Staci with Taylor.

But here's the problem, how can I go to a football game if I'm in *One Stepp Closer?* I'll have to abide by the rules or convince my parents that I'm better and don't need to be in there anymore. I don't have time right now to come up with a plan because when I look out my window, we're pulling into the driveway of Overlook Cemetery.

* * *

Rosie is still stuck to my side like glue as everyone who came to say their last goodbyes stand around the open gravesite. Staci's casket is propped on some metal pipes sticking out of the ground.

I pretty much keep my head down because looking at the closed casket isn't an option. I made it this far, but saying goodbye to her makes it too final, and I'm not ready for that. I want to keep her alive for as long as I can.

One by one, each person that is standing around the gravesite walks up to Staci's casket and places a white rose on the top. Before I know it, my mom touches my shoulder indicating that the service is over and it's time for us to go to the gathering at Mr. and Mrs. Garrison's house. When I look up, I'm the last one left standing here. I place my rose on the top and walk away.

I've noticed that my mom seems different somehow—more fragile then I remember. I'm so used to her being away from the house and always busy working that this person beside me seems new and actually…loveable.

Does it have something to do with the letter I wrote? It does seem possible because I mentioned in there that we weren't a family that shares love. I'm not sure what it is, but I like the person she is with me now.

It comes to me that she wouldn't be this person if I didn't do what I did to get to the place we're at now. Does suicide have that effect on people? But then I think that I am her child and she loves me no matter what. That she has always loved me, but never knew how to show me that she did.

* * *

The day turns out to be beautiful with blue skies and a golden medallion sun shining down on us. Unlike my grandpa's funeral where it had rained all day. It was like the clouds were crying for his loss, which surprises me that it's nice outside today because I don't feel happy inside and full of sunshine and warmth.

As I look up at the sky, my skin starts to feel warm from the sun, something I haven't experienced in days.

We left the cemetery, driving towards Mrs. G's house for a family and friend get-together. Another farewell gathering I'm not looking forward to. We stop at our house so my mom can grab the food that she prepared, but I stay in the car as we're not staying long.

We are back on the road again as I try to find the words to tell my parents that I don't really want to go, and if we could just skip the social function, but the words never come out of my mouth. Before I know it, we're parking along the side of the street across from Staci's house.

Staci's parents live in a two-story, Victorian style house from the eighteen-fifties. They restored the house after buying it sixteen years ago from some old lady who lived in it. Mrs. G loves telling the story whenever someone talks about how much they love the house.

I take in a deep breath and swallow before opening the door and climbing out of the car. I'm just praying that I'll keep it together and not lose my mind or say something I shouldn't. I will be in Staci's house, breathing in Staci's smell, and looking at Staci's pictures all over the walls.

I look down when Rosie clasps her hand into mine. I smile at her, and she gives me a look like a frightened puppy surrounded by wolves. She's still worried about what I'll do. What I've already tried to do to myself; something I know I can't ever undo.

I crouch down so we're eye-to-eye. "I love you, Rosie, and I'm so sorry about what I did. Please don't worry about me, okay?" I whisper. I had to just tell her I'm sorry, but she still doesn't leave my side.

She tries hard to smile back at me, but I know it's forced. She'll forgive me in time, right? I pray she does, and make a promise to myself to make it up to her. I have to make it up to her.

Once my mom joins us at the side of the car, we all walk up the driveway to the front door that's open as people gather inside carrying glass containers of food for everyone. My mom brought her famous meatloaf that I love so much, and think to myself, how long has it been since I've actually eaten?

We filter into the kitchen where my mom sets her glass dish on the table already heaping with food. There has to be at least twenty-some people here and more making their way inside.

Part of me wants to sneak up to Staci's room, but the other half of me is petrified. What if I see where she hung herself, though I'm not sure where exactly she did it? A chill runs through my body just like they say happens when a ghost is near. The hairs on my arm stand up and my body shivers. I could actually see her haunting this house, haunting me.

Rosie finally lets go of my hand and makes her way to our mother who's talking to the principal of the school. Part of me wants to know what they're talking about, but then again I don't.

I look around the room; no one is looking at me, which makes me relax. I make my way towards the hallway by the kitchen and up the back stairwell before anyone knows I'm gone.

Once I'm upstairs, I take small steps as I make my way down the hall to the last door on the left. Her room faces the backyard where we used to play on the swing set that's still there. I wonder if they will ever get rid of that thing.

I stop once I'm at her door; it's closed. I reach out and place my hand on the cold metal knob. I have to fight back the tears that want to come rushing out of me. I take in a breath and hold it as I turn the knob and push the door forward. I was waiting for the squeak the hinges make whenever the door is being opened, but they must have oiled them in the past few weeks since I've been here.

Light beams in through the blinds, landing on her pink chiffon comforter. Staci had loved the color pink ever since we were eight years old. You'd think once she became a teenager, she'd pitch out the comforter and get something more grown-up, but that was Staci.

Talk To Me

Everything in her room looks untouched, just the way I remember it. She was the organized freak, and I was the slob friend. Two perfect people meant to stay friends for a lifetime. Although, I was expecting us to live way into our eighties or nineties, not our teens.

I sit on the edge of the bed, and then lay back. I close my eyes, soaking in the scent of her. It doesn't take long before tears find their way out, and I'm sobbing like a baby.

I roll onto my side and hug my knees in close. "I miss you so much," I whisper into the empty room.

"I miss her too," Staci's mom replies.

I jolt up and off the bed, my heart beating fast. "I'm sorry," I say. "I know I shouldn't be in here."

"Don't be sorry, Carly. I know how much you loved her. She loved you too. You have every right to be in her room."

I bow my head, trying to hide the tears that keep pouring out. That's when I feel Mrs. G in front of me. "What did you mean, you know who killed her?" she asks.

I stiffen. *Shit, shit, shit,* I think to myself. I know I have to tell her something. She's not the kind of person to back down. She'll find a way to get things out of me, and I don't know if I'm strong enough to hide the secret.

"Carly…" she pauses. "You wouldn't have said something if there wasn't a reason for saying it. Do you know what made her want to kill herself? Please tell me. I need to know why," she pleads. Tears are running down her face. Her eyeliner has smeared under both eyes. It seems like a senseless thing to wear when you know you're going to be crying.

I bite my lower lip, trying to find a way around this. I have to lie to her because saying something on a day like today is just wrong. She's mourning—we all are—and I need to find a solution to our problem.

"I'm sorry; I didn't mean for it to sound that way Mrs. G. I was just mad and wanted to blame someone for Staci taking her…" I stop because I don't want to say the words. I can't say the words.

Her eyes stare into mine. I don't know if she believes me or not, but I hope she does even though I know it didn't sound very convincing.

"Carly, please," she says again.

"I'm sorry, Mrs. G; I shouldn't have said what I did. I didn't mean anything by it," I reply, looking her in the eye this time.

Her shoulders sag, feeling defeated. I know exactly what that feels like. I do the only thing I know what to do, and that's opening my arms and pulling her into me. Mrs. G was always handing out hugs when I came over, which was almost every weekend. Now it's my turn to return the favor.

I feel her start to shake in my embrace, and I'm trying hard not to join in. We'd be two hysterical females up here in this room. The room I've spent more nights in than I can count.

I'm not sure how much time has passed when I hear a knock on the door. We both let go and Mrs. G is wiping away the tears and smearing the rest of her make-up.

I look towards the doorway and see Mr. G standing there. “Hey, Carly. How are you doing?” he asks, looking just as sad and miserable, if not worse, than Mrs. G.

“I’m okay,” I say. God, I feel so terrible for them. This shouldn’t have happened. I should have gone to Staci after what happened to me, but I didn’t and now she took her own life because I didn’t stop her, I didn’t help her. Then I hear a low whisper. It was so faint that I almost missed it. “It’s not your fault.” I hear and look frantically around the room.

“Carly, are you okay? You look frightened,” Mrs. G questions.

“What?” I turn and see both of them looking at me. “I’m fine, just don’t feel so good,” I say, which isn’t a total lie.

“Please, sit down,” she motions to the bed. “Sometimes it helps by placing your head between your legs. Makes the dizziness go away. You know Staci always had dizzy spells, and she…” Mrs. G stops. I hear a whimper. “Sorry,” she says and runs out of the room. Mr. G gives me a reassuring smile before chasing after her.

I don’t blame Mrs. G one bit for crying. I’m actually surprised she was able to get out of bed today. I would’ve been sick to my stomach with grief. I am sick with sadness, but not enough to keep me from going to the funeral, or was it more my mom's doing rather than mine?

I hadn't realized until now that I'm left by myself in the room when I hear the same faint whisper, but this time it says, "Help Jessica."

This can't be happening.
I'm fucking losing my mind.

(S)

13 | Room

I quickly stand and spin around as if I'm looking for someone, but there's no one here. I'll be honest with you; I have never believed in ghosts and the thought of Staci haunting me is downright freaky. No, it's not real, I don't believe in that stuff—so there's no way she's here and that I heard her voice.

That's when the door to the room slams shut, and I'm standing here about ready to pee in my pants or dress because I'm not wearing jeans.

"Carly," the voice whispers. "Don't be afraid. It's not like I can hurt you."

My eyes trace the room from top-to-bottom and side-to-side, but I don't see anything or anyone. Not even a bright light or a glimmer of Staci floating. But like I said, I don't believe in ghosts so it must be the lack of food or sleep or something because this isn't real. I need to go back downstairs and tell my parents to take me home because I'm starting to lose it big time!

"Stop!" the voice exclaims. "Please, Carly, don't run. Help Jessica before it's too late." The voice is more demanding this time and I decide to find out if it's really her—really Staci.

"Okay," I say, "if this is my best friend Staci, then you'll need to prove it to me." The room falls silent. "If it's really you, Staci, then make something move in this room." Nothing. I shake my head and walk to the door. My eyes sketch over every inch of the room, waiting for something, anything to move, but nothing does. I wait one more second before I leave and close the door to her room, knowing that it might just be the last time I will ever be in it.

* * *

I take the same stairs as I did coming up, which brings me back to the kitchen area. When I enter the room, I see Mick and Alisha standing by the chips and dip. I walk over as if nothing is different.

"Hey," Mick says. "We were wondering where you went."

"I had to use the bathroom," I lied.

"Are you hungry?" Alisha asks, her eyes tracing the length of my body.

It doesn't take a genius to see how thin I've gotten. Although, I don't ever recall her looking as thin as she does now. She wasn't fat or anything before I went away, and she definitely isn't even close to being fat now. It's almost like we are competing against one another.

I nod and grab a plate beside her. I start shoveling spoonfuls of pasta salad and my mom's famous meatloaf on my plate.

"Are you seriously going to eat all that?" Mick asks.

I look down at my plate that is loaded with food and place the spoon back in the pan. "Yeah," I reply, though I'm not sure if I can eat it all. It's been days since I've eaten actual food. I'm not sure if my stomach can handle it.

I grab a plastic fork and lean against the counter next to Mick. I can feel them watching me as I lift the fork to my mouth and start to chew the meatloaf. I can feel my throat tighten, and I look around for something to wash the food down. I casually walk to the counter opposite of where we are standing, and I set the plate down and grab a bottle of water. As I try to swallow the water, the meatloaf in my throat feels lodged, and I'm afraid I might puke. I swallow again, and finally the food goes down my throat. This is going to be harder than I thought.

"Are you okay?" Alisha asks. "You don't look so good."

I empty the bottle of water and grab another one. The last thing I want is to have my friends see me this way. I look over at Mick and Alisha who are both staring at me with worried eyes. I feel like crying, but I can't do that in front of them. That's when I see *him* standing in the next room, talking with my dad. He has a smug look on his face as if he's KING of the world. Shit, what if he tells him we've been broken up and my parents ask me about it? I can't tell them what happened, even though I should.

Both Mick and Alisha follow my gaze. I hadn't told anyone except Staci that Taylor and I had broken up. But, I know Mick isn't stupid and he can figure things out. Or maybe, he had weeks ago, since I didn't talk about Taylor like I used to or at all, for that matter.

My stomach flips and I know that if I don't get out of here I will vomit everywhere. Both Mick and Alisha come to my side and escort me to the kitchen door, which leads to the backyard. Once we're outside, all three of us sit down on the stairs. Alisha advices me to put my head between my legs just like Mrs. G did.

It actually works, and I start to feel like myself again.

"Do you want to talk about what's going on with you and Taylor?" Mick asks.

I shake my head.

"Alisha and I are both here for you if you need someone to talk to," Mick replies.

I think to myself, *when did they become a couple?* I guess a lot has happened since my days in *One Stepp Closer*.

Alisha sits quietly, as usual, like she does at lunchtime, but when I think that we will all just sit here and not speak, she speaks.

"We know you're not together anymore, you and Taylor. We also know that Staci was seeing him before she…" Alisha pauses. I know she doesn't want to say the words that were about to come next.

She sucks in a breath and then blows it out before continuing, "Mick and I have seen him with Jessica at the football games. We also heard he's taking her to the Homecoming Dance in two weeks. We just thought you should know before…"

I stop her from saying what I think she was about to say by turning away from her. The words were on the edge of her tongue. There's no way that they know what happened to me or to Staci. I never told anyone.

Part of me wants to ask Alisha to say what she was about to say and get it over with, but then if the words are spoken, does it make it true? Does it become more real? Will it release everything I hold inside? I don't think I could handle it if everyone knew what happened to me.

"Carly, there you are," my father says behind us. "Your mom's about ready to take you home and then back to *One Stepp Closer.*"

My shoulders sag; I don't want to leave, but I also don't want to walk back in the house past all those people and Taylor.

"We'll walk with you, Carly," Mick suggests.

"Yeah, we'll be right beside you," Alisha says.

I look at Mick and then Alisha. "Okay, thank you," I whisper.

Mick stands first, then it's Alisha who helps me up and puts her arm around my waist as if she knows I need her help standing, which I do.

We walk back inside, and I say goodbye to Mr. and Mrs. G before I walk straight out the front door and to my parents' car. I turn around before opening the back-passenger door and climbing inside.

There were two things at that moment that made me scream. The first, was Taylor standing beside the house staring right at me. And the second, was when I saw the curtain move in the upstairs window. It wasn't Staci's room; hers was on the other side of the house.

This window was in the attic where Staci and I always played and shared our deepest and darkest secrets. I now know where she hung herself because I can see her through the window, hanging from the rafters.

I have totally lost my mind.
I need to get outta here.
I want to go home.

Or maybe to *One Stepp Closer* because I'm one step closer to nutsville.

(R)

14 | Story

I didn't get a choice after what I'd seen; my parents took me straight to the crazy house. That's what they should call it anyway because now I'm far from being *One Stepp Closer* to getting out of this place.

I wish you could've seen their faces after what I told them I saw in the upstairs window. Now that I'm sedated and strapped to the bed, I feel sorry for what I did right in front of Rosie. She's never going to get over this tragedy. Mom will have to start sending her to a therapist before she becomes just like me.

No one has been allowed in my room since I came back all hysterical. I'm not even sure how many days have gone by before I see Jordan and Becki walk past my room, heading to the morning meeting, which I'm not able to attend for a couple more days. The doctors think I need to clear my mind because they think going to Staci's funeral is what triggered me to see something that wasn't really there. I know that's true because I had just seen her in the casket. So I know she wasn't actually hanging from the rafters.

* * *

It was late afternoon when my shrink came into my room. Since I'm not going to the group meetings, they come to me.

Just minutes before the nurse assigned to my room came in and took out the IV they used to administer the drug for sedation. It makes me feel mellow; I could actually live on this stuff. No more worries or pain. Life would be great.

Dr. Gerald Mills is my psychiatrist and he loves to talk, even though I'm the one who's supposed to be talking.

"Talk to me, Carly," he says. "Trust me, it will help you feel better and there's no reason to keep these thoughts to yourself. Once you release them, you'll be yourself again."

Doubtful, I think to myself. There is no way I'm going to tell him what happened to me. It's not like you can make me talk, but maybe he's right; maybe I would feel better.

"Carly, let me tell you a story about what happened to me when I was younger. It's one of the reasons why I became a psychiatrist. I had to be eight or nine years old at the time. My friend and I were playing a game of hide-and-seek. When I found him, he was in my parents' closet. He was holding my dad's gun and pointing it at me; then, for some reason he decided to point the gun at himself as if he was looking down the barrel and pulled the trigger, not knowing it was loaded.

"My mom, who was home at the time, came running into the room. When she saw that my friend had shot himself in the throat and all the blood on the floor, she started to scream, then ran to the phone in the bedroom and called 9-1-1. I've had to live with this since I was young, watching my friend die in front of me, knowing there was nothing I could do to save him. I remember being in a state of shock. I didn't cry; I didn't scream. I just stood there watching him and knowing I'd never be the same again. It's one of the reasons why I'm a psychiatrist because I want to help people get past tragedies in their lives. I want to help you get past whatever happened to you and your friend so you can leave here and live the life you're supposed to live."

My mouth falls open, stunned by what he'd just said. If I had been there with Staci when she died, I'd never be me again. But there's more than her killing herself for the reason why I'm here. Maybe it's time to tell someone, or maybe I should just keep it to myself. I don't know the right or wrong thing to do. I just know that I need to get out of here and save someone else before the same thing happens to them. I also wonder why Dr. Mills thinks something else bad had to happen for me to be in here.

The clock ticks by and before I know it, Dr. Mills stands and leaves the room. I never gave him the chance to help me.

* * *

The same nurse comes back in the room and unbuckles the restraints around my wrists and ankles.

"You can go to the cafeteria for dinner now," she says.

I know I look shocked, but that's because I am. The minute she leaves my room, I rub my wrists to get the feeling back into my hands and arms. They had me in a gown so I quickly change and make my way out the door and down the hall towards the cafeteria.

As soon as I appear in the doorway, everyone goes quiet and their eyes are on me. I hate being the center of attention. I must have been out of control when my parents brought me back here or there'd be no reason for them to be looking at me. I don't remember exactly what happened.

I walk over to the table where Becki and the rest of the gang are sitting. At first, no one says anything, then Becki asks how I'm feeling.

"I'm good, just shocked that they let me out of my room. Thought I'd be there until they released me or I died, whichever came first," I chuckle a little, but no one laughs back.

"So, how are all of you?" I ask. Everyone looks at each other and then back at me. "Okay, what's going on? Why are all of you looking at me like I just killed someone? Somebody talk to me!" My voice rises with each word.

Becki clears her throat, "We saw you when you came in a few days ago."

"Yeah," Jordan says. "You were screaming and pulling your hair out," she said in a sympathetic voice.

My right hand automatically flies to my head, and I can feel a bald spot that once had hair. I hadn't even looked in the mirror before coming here, and now I feel embarrassed. I look at the others sitting at the table; all but three have their heads down eating their meals.

Gabby leans over and whispers in my ear, "I'm a good listener if you want to talk about what happened."

Talk To Me

I've liked Gabby since the day I met her, which wasn't that long ago. Although, I didn't really know her, there was just something there that I liked about her. Something that I can't explain.

I can't keep the truth to myself much longer.
Maybe I should talk.
Put an end to my misery.

(A)

15 | Don't Touch Me

Two weeks have passed since my breakdown and my best friend's funeral. I've been going to group meetings and have been meeting with Dr. Mills, but not with my approval.

In this place, you don't get a choice. You either follow the rules or pay the consequences. This means you are confined to your room with no freedom of the game-room lounge or food in the cafeteria. Dr. Mills has to come every day for one hour whether we talk or not. "Whatever," I mumble to myself. "It's his time wasted, not mine."

The morning nurse comes in and as usual, I get my weight checked. They calculated me at eighty-nine pounds when I first was brought in, and then it went down from there. My lowest was seventy-six pounds, which was after Staci's funeral. Now, two weeks later, I'm at ninety-seven.

Nurse Angelia said she'd like to see me at one hundred and five before I'm released, which she said could be in the next week or two; since I've been abiding by the rules, I'll get an early release.

I smile at her thin, unflawed face. I'm not sure how old she is, but she doesn't look much older than thirty. She wears her hair half in a bun and half in a ponytail; *messy bun* is what I call it. Sometimes I catch Dr. Mills eyeing Nurse Angelia when they cross each other's path. I don't think either one of them is married. Dr. Mills isn't all that bad looking, but still I think Nurse Angelia can do better.

All of us are in the game lounge, and for the first time in a couple of days, I'm playing ping-pong. No one wants to play with me since they found out how good I am.

Today I'm playing Scott, but that's because we haven't played the game together before. I end up getting the final point and win the game. I cheer and shout, "Don't be such a sore loser," as I'm laughing at Scott.

Before today, I'd never seen Scott in a bad mood so it startled me when he got mad at me, and the next thing I know, he has me pinned down on the couch and is straddled on top of me, clamping his hand over my mouth to keep me from speaking or screaming. I squeeze my eyes shut and flashbacks come rushing in and I see Taylor; he's… he's got me pinned down in the front seat of his car.

He was pissed off from losing the football game, just like last week, but tonight was different. Tonight, he was in a mood I hadn't seen before.

It had been hot and muggy out all night. So when we got in his car, I thought for sure he'd turn on the A/C before driving me home. But we just sat there in his car as if waiting for everyone to leave the parking lot.

I knew he didn't want to sit in traffic, always shouting obscene words at other people because we weren't moving or the other driver did something stupid which was all the time, according to Taylor.

So we were sitting there in the dark hot car, waiting for what I didn't know. I was about to say something to him, but that's when he pinned me against the passenger door and pressed his sweaty, sticky body against me.

He forced his lips against mine as he wrapped an arm behind me and laid me flat on the front seat. He reached down, ripped off my panties from under my skirt, and said that I wanted this; that I deserved what he was about to do to me.

I started to scream and say no, but then his hand clamped over my mouth as he forced himself in me, pounding me fast and hard like I was some kind of rag doll that he could just man-handle.

The pain was so sharp and intense that I could feel the skin around my vagina ripping, and it made tears escape from the corner of my eyes.

I tried to scream out for him to stop and that he was hurting me. I tried to push him off, but I couldn't get my hands between us because my one arm was pinned down and the other was twisted under my body weight.

When he finished, I begged again for him to get off of me, "Taylor, please stop!" I cried out over and over as he removed his hand from my mouth. Once he was off of me, I quickly scooted towards the passenger side door, hugging my arms around my body.

Minutes passed when I finally realized that I needed to get out of the fucking car and away from him. Before I could open the door, he said, "Don't even think about it. You get out of the car and I will fucking kill you. If you even think of telling anyone, I will kill you and your family. So sit the fuck down and I'll take you home. I don't need your parents thinking anything happened," he hissed. "You will keep your mouth shut because I have a lot of people watching my games for a chance at a scholarship. Do you fucking understand? If one word of this gets out, it will be over. My whole life will be over!"

I sat there huddled against the passenger door, waiting and praying to be out of his car and away from him. When I finally got home, I hoped my parents wouldn't see me come in the house.

But I couldn't be so lucky. Both of my parents were watching TV so I said goodnight and quickly went to my bedroom. It hurt so bad to walk, but once in my room, I locked the door and slowly went into the bathroom that was connected to my room. I locked that door as well, afraid that someone would walk in on me. I took off my clothes, and that's when I saw blood all over my skirt and down my leg, but I was thankful that my parents hadn't looked at me when I came home. I felt panic flow through me, but knew I had to keep it together and climbed in the shower to wash away the filth, his filth.

That night and every night afterward, I couldn't stop him from entering my dreams. Or should I say, my nightmares.

Then, I'm brought back to the present time when I hear Becki yelling, "Get the fuck off of her, Scott!"

But I still feel the weight on top of me.

"Damn it, Scott, get off of her; she's freaking out!" Jordan yells.

Then, I'm free from the weight and there's no more yelling. It's no longer hot or muggy around me, and when I open my eyes, everyone is looking at me with fear in their eyes and on their faces. Now they know what happened to me. What Taylor did to me.

Taylor raped me!
Taylor raped Staci.
And I know he'll do it again to someone else.

(P)

16 | Dr. Mills

Now I know why I've become so bitter and angry towards people and things. It's not like me to be mean and rude towards others, but what Taylor did to me changed who I once was. I don't know if I'll ever be that once polite and popular girl again, but I don't think I even care about that anymore.

I'm sitting in a chair in Dr. Mills's office. He's sitting across from me writing in his notepad. I don't know if it was because of Scott holding me down that made me finally want to talk. I know when he had me pinned down; I felt the horror all over again. I know I'll never be the same, but at least I won't have to hold it inside anymore.

They called my parents, but only my mom shows up because someone needs to watch Rosie. She enters the room and sits down on the sofa next to me. I have the choice to stay or leave; I choose to stay and listen to what Dr. Mills is about to share with my mom. Before she arrived, he asked if I would allow him to include my mother in the patient/doctor confidentiality and tell her what happened so I can get the help I need.

I agreed. Dr. Mills had me sign a paper to show that I allowed this *"inclusion,"* as he called it. It was okay with me.

Dr. Mills goes over what happened to me earlier in the game room, and then without hesitation, informs my mom about the rape. The moment he says the word *rape,* I can see her stiffen, and then she turns towards me. I can see tears streaming down her face.

She reaches out for me and pulls me into her arms. I feel like I'm her baby again. Little and fragile, wishing I'd told her or someone sooner, then maybe Staci would still be here. Why is it that I can forget what I've been through and only think of my best friend who is no longer here? And that she would have endured the same brutal act as I did.

Dr. Mills insists that I go to the hospital for a rape kit to be done and then go from there. He says I should press charges against Taylor before he does this to someone else. That's when I tell them that I think he raped Staci too and that's why she killed herself. And I know in order to help Jessica, I need to mention her name too, but I don't. I figure if they're going to arrest Taylor then she won't have to worry about him doing that to her, unless… Unless he has already done it.

"Jessica," I whisper her name into the room. "You need to help save Jessica from him."

"Jessica who? Is he going… Has he…?" my mom asks as if pleading.

"I don't know, but you can ask Mick or Alisha from school or I can ask them," I reply.

My mom pulls my phone out of her purse and hands it to me. "Call them so we can stop this from happening to another girl," she insists. Dr. Mills nods his head in agreement for me to call them.

I call Mick and he answers on the second ring. After we say "hello" and get the "how are you doing" out of the way, I ask him if he knows a "Jessica" and I get her last name. I hang up and Dr. Mills picks up his phone on the desk and talks to his secretary who's sitting on the other side of the door.

Twenty minutes later, my mom and I are in the car and she's driving me to the hospital where a police officer is waiting for me—for us.

My mom is holding my hand the whole way; I start to cry, and feel scared and terrified all over again. I don't know what will happen to me once we go in, but I'm glad that I have my mom next to me, protecting me, and wish she had been there the night Taylor took my innocence.

My mind flashes back to that awful night again. The weight of his body on me. My head being pressed against the side panel of the passenger door, I couldn't move.

I suck in quick breaths because I can still feel the pain.

Taylor took something that I will never get back.

I'm so scared.
Can I do this?
Can I let the doctor examine?

(E)

17 | Hospital

Once inside the hospital, a nurse takes us to a room where they have me change into a gown. I have never been in this part of a hospital before so I'm not sure what to expect. After I change, the nurse orders me to lie down on the bed and that she'll be back in with the doctor.

My mom is out in the hall talking to a police officer about what happened. I can't hear what they are talking about, but I'm sure I already know since I'm the victim.

The nurse and doctor return to the room, my mom following behind them. The doctor goes over what is going to be done to me, but informs my mom that she will need to wait outside until they are finished collecting the evidence, if there still is any.

The doctor, a middle-aged, dark-haired woman who looks to be around my mom's age, goes over the procedure again with the nurse and me. I think because she feels my fear. She assures me that it will be quick and somewhat painless, but if it should hurt me in any way to let her know.

She also informs me that she's going to do a pregnancy test. I hadn't even thought about possibly getting pregnant. God, what would I do if I was? Would I keep the baby or get rid of it? I don't want to think about having a baby. I'm only fifteen years old; I'm not ready to have a baby, to be a mom.

Tears start to slide down my face and the doctor hasn't even started examining me yet.

"Carly, are you okay?" the doctor asks.

I sniffle a cry, "I don't want to be pregnant."

"Carly, I didn't say you were, but we still need to do a test to make sure. I know you said it's been at least five weeks since the rape, but it still doesn't hurt to check. Today's technology can show a pregnancy within the first week of conception," the doctor informs me.

I nod and say, "Okay."

* * *

I'm not sure how much time has passed before the doctor is finished with the examination and my mom's allowed back in the room.

I was thankful it wasn't as painful as I imagined it would be. I didn't care much for the cold metal tool that she inserted into me. The whole embarrassing exam is over, and I pray that I don't have to go through it again. It just made me feel gross and ashamed.

Before leaving, the doctor said I could get dressed and that it would take a few days for the results to come back. I was released to go home with my mom.

Once we pull into the driveway, I feel a panic attack coming on, but I'm not sure why since I got what I wanted and I'm now home.

My dad greets us at the door with Rosie standing behind him. He gives me a hug, though he is hesitant at first, probably feeling weird or ashamed by what happened to me. I'm sure my mom told him when the doctor was with me.

When I see Rosie, I kneel down and wrap my arms around her. I missed her so much it hurts. Besides, I want to make it up to her for what I did. I still think she deserves a better sister than me.

After we eat dinner, I go to my room, which has been cleaned since the last time I was here, and sit on my bed with my back resting against the headboard.

I go onto my phone and tap the Instagram icon. First, I see this photo of me that I don't ever remember taking. Second, I don't know how anyone found out, but there are several, no, hundreds of comments about what happened to me. Kids at my school are calling me a liar and a *ho'*. That, if it's true, then I deserved what happened. One says, "I shouldn't go around accusing people of rape if I allowed it to happen," but I didn't allow him to do it, he forced himself on me and raped me.

Tears slide down my face and I can't stop crying. There's no way I can go back to school if my classmates are going to call me names. I know what they do to other kids. I've seen it with my own eyes.

The next comment that pops on the screen says that it's all my fault Staci killed herself because I didn't want to be her friend anymore. More comments are added and they don't stop:

> ***jenna_mellow commented: "Did you hear about Taylor Ryans getting arrested?"***

paigesummit commented: "No, what did he do?"

jenna_mellow commented: "Carly Boyles is saying that he raped her."

gavinhangger commented: "No way! That can't be true."

camfasker commented: "He's the captain of the football team, he doesn't need to rape a girl to have sex with him, they are flaunting themselves at him all the time."

paigesummit commented: "She's such a BITCH."

alishagiller commented: "Maybe she got what she had coming to her."

russellasher commented: "Yeah, she so deserved it."

paigesummit commented: "She's such a liar. I bet that's why Staci killed herself. She couldn't handle being around a slut like Carly."

jenna_mellow commented: "I bet she slept with the whole football team. They better watch it or she'll say they raped her too, lol."

camfasker commented: "Yeah, she better shut her fucking mouth before we shut it for her."

The comments keep coming one after another, and just as I'm about to the throw my phone across the room, my mom walks in and sees me crying.

"Carly, what's wrong?" She walks quickly to the side of the bed and sits down next to me. I hand her my phone. She sits there reading every word they have to say. I can see her getting upset. This wasn't supposed to happen, but it's what I knew would happen and that's why I didn't say anything to begin with.

My mom starts typing something on my phone. She must be replying to their comments, and I'll be harassed even more because my *mommy* is standing up for me.

When she's done, she hands the phone back to me, and says, "Let me know if there's any more problems; I'll handle it."

I look down at my phone and read what she has written:

> ***"I have each and every one of your contact information now, so if you continue to harass my daughter, I will press charges against you and your family for bullying and harassing my daughter who is innocent in all of this. She didn't ask for any of this to happen, Taylor forced himself on her without her permission! Does anyone want to leave a comment now?"***

My lips form a smile, and I wrap my arms around her. She's my savior. I would have never guessed that she would be there for me when I needed her the most. I had thought she was too busy with work to be my mom. I guess I had gotten her all wrong. She's the greatest person I know, and I should've gone to her sooner before any of this happened. But I can't change the past, even though I want my best friend back. Someone sure got it right when they said, "Life isn't fair."

Getting better.
Though, I'm still not myself.
Will I ever get through this?

(D)

18 | School

My mom keeps me out of school the rest of the week and now it's the following Monday. I'm up early and dressed for school. My mom said she would be taking me because we have a meeting with the Guidance Counselor this morning.

The moment we walk into the school, all faces are on me. Kids I didn't even know are looking at me. I feel like my name is tattooed on my forehead or possibly a sign on my back. I can hear the whispers as we walk by them. I so don't want to be here right now or ever for that matter.

Once we're in the office, my mom signs in and we take a seat against the wall. The woman behind the desk named Joanne says it will be a few minutes.

I take out my cell phone and check for any messages, but there are none. Mick hasn't even sent me a text since I saw him last, and I wonder what he's been up to lately. He's been my only friend since Staci.

"Mrs. Boyles," a man says from the doorway.

We both look up and I see Mr. Davis my Guidance Counselor standing in front of us. We follow him to his office near the back and to the left. Even though I've been in his office a couple of times for scheduling my classes, it still looks small and cramped. He seriously needs to learn some organizational skills.

My mom and I take a seat next to each other, which there really isn't any choice. There are only two seats in the room besides Mr. Davis's chair. He closes the door before sitting down at his desk.

My mom jumps right in and tells him everything that has happened and that she will not hesitate to fight for justice. She told him of the hateful comments on my Instagram page and that this needs to stop.

"I completely understand your thoughts and feelings on the matter and I—I mean, *we*—at Lakeport Central will make sure that things don't get out of hand and that Carly is safe here at this school. We have a ***no-bullying*** policy here and we will enforce the rules, if needed," Mr. Davis concludes.

My mom nods. "Oh, I'll make sure that you do so," she assures him.

The moment she says the words, I lift my head and look at him. His face is flushed by her words. He's literary scared of her, and I love it. My mom, my savior, but I know the kids outside these walls won't be so…*what's the word I'm trying to think of?* Kind, caring, considerate, loving, thoughtful; perhaps even forgiving?—there's so many words that they *could use*, but I know they'll all be cruel and still say nasty things to me, about me.

* * *

My mom leaves and I head to my locker to retrieve the books I need for class. The first thing I see when I get to my locker is the words *liar* and *slut* written across my locker door. Everyone around me gets quiet as I put in my combination, turn the dial, and open my locker. I grab the books I need, close the door, and make my way to Math class.

The first thing my eyes do when I enter the room is find Staci's chair. The one I wish she was still sitting in. I go to my assigned seat and place my Math book on the desk. I think if I just sit here and look straight ahead, then no one will pay any attention to me and maybe forget I exist—doubtful, but wishful thinking.

I feel a tap on my shoulder, and then another one. That's when I realize I have my head nestled on my arm on the desk. I had fallen asleep.

My head jolts up and it's my teacher, Mrs. Elmer, standing next to me. I look around and there's no one else in the room. How did I not hear the bell ring?

"I'm sorry, Mrs. Elmer. I didn't realize I'd fallen asleep. I'm…" Mrs. Elmer interrupts me.

"Carly, there's no need to apologize. I was informed about what happened and… well, I'm here if you need someone to talk to," she smiles at me.

I wasn't sure what to think about her offer. Actually, the thought of talking to Mrs. Elmer is not and wouldn't be my first choice. She's my teacher, not my friend, though I can't say I actually have many, if any, friends now. I haven't even seen Mick since I came back to school this morning, but we really don't have any classes together except lunch, although it's not actually a class.

"Thank you, I'll keep that in mind," I reply and gather my things and leave the classroom.

I'm thankful as the minutes tick by and lunch arrives. Not so much as to eat, but I really want to see Mick. As usual, I stop at my locker before lunch so I don't have to come back this way, and the words are no longer written across my locker. I grab my books and practically sprint to the cafeteria.

It's funny how sometimes you forget things and maybe even think that whatever happened was actually all a dream. That you could just go on with your life and pretend that nothing else matters. That people will just forget about the past and treat you as they should.

Really, who am I kidding, right? This is high school, and these kids have no clue how to respect other people. They are only thinking of themselves as I used to do. But, I know a lot has happened, has changed in the past month, and I'm not who I used to be. They are not who they used to be. I was raped, and Staci was raped and she ended up killing herself, and I tried to kill myself. How is all this fair? How did I become the person I am now? Angry and bitter.

Half the kids here didn't even talk to me before; now, they want to say shit about me and call me names. How did I become the bad person, when all I wanted to do was escape the pain I was feeling inside from Taylor raping me? I just wanted to be loved by a boy, not attacked, and left to pretend it never happened. He threatened me and said he'd kill my family if I said anything. I wonder if he threatened Staci too? How is someone supposed to forget and act like it never happened?

I'm standing in the entrance of the lunchroom and as if I'd made a huge noise or screamed bloody murder, all eyes are on me. I haven't done anything and yet I'm the center of attention.

The room falls silent except for the clanking the servers are making, serving food to the students. I swallow and make my way to my table where Mick, Alisha, and I sit, but there's no one sitting there.

I glance around the room and my eyes stop on Alisha who's sitting with Gavin, Jenna, Paige, Russell, and Cam who are all in my Biology class, and the ones who were saying shit about me on Instagram.

Alisha is sitting with the popular kids, and Mick is nowhere in sight. I had thought that they were dating when I saw them at Staci's funeral, but I guess I was wrong.

The quiet Alisha I knew is laughing and talking with the group she's now sitting with. What the hell happened since I've been gone?

Instead of sitting by myself and having everyone looking at me, I turn and leave the cafeteria. I can hear the words of several kids calling me a ho', a slut, and a liar behind my back.

I hold back the tears that want to come pouring out and quickly walk down the hall to the library. I don't want anyone to see me cry; that'll just give them more fuel for the fire.

Part of me wants to run out of the school and never come back, but that's what they want. It would make them think that they won and that they can talk about anyone they want. That bullying other people will make them more superior, but what it really does is take the focus off them. So no one will see their faults, their mistakes.

Stupid kids.
Makes me think of killing myself again.
I wish I was dead.
Fuck this school!

(M)

19 | Jessica

I slide between the six-foot high rows of mystery and romance novels. I used to love a good romance book, but my love life is definitely not something worth talking about at the moment. So, I stick to the shelves on my left.

My eyes follow the titles of the books. I don't have a book in mind, as I haven't really cared about reading lately. I pull out a book, glance at the cover. There's a headstone with the name Michaels on it, and an open book sitting on the dirt where the person was just buried. The book is entitled *"Hidden Secrets,"* which sounds intriguing. I flip the book over in my hand to read the summary and I'm hooked; and so I carry it to a small cushioned chair in the corner of the room.

The library has several tables and some chairs that you'd normally see in a café or someplace like Barnes and Noble. I sit down and look around the room before opening the book.

I'm not sure how long I was sitting there when a shadow covers the pages I'm reading.

I look up to see a girl with long red wavy hair and the greenest eyes I've ever seen. I'm not trying to sound like I'm hitting on her or anything, but she is pretty.

The girl stands there not saying a word. I'm waiting for her to start calling me names, but she doesn't say anything. Seconds pass and she still stands there staring down at me.

I close the book and place it in my lap. "Is there something wrong?" I say, looking at the chair in front of me.

"You're Carly, right?" she asks.

"Yeah, what's it to you?" I snap, not caring if I'm being loud and rude.

"You dated Taylor, Taylor Ryans?"

I swallow. I wasn't sure if I was ready for a conversation about him. I nod because I can't find the words I want to say. I nearly pull the muscle in my neck as I whip my head up at her when she speaks again.

"I'm Jessica," she whispers.

I swallow again to keep the bile down. My stomach tightens thankful that I haven't eaten lunch yet. *"Help Jessica"* replays in my head as if Staci is whispering her name in my ear.

"By the look on your face and the words you're not speaking, I assume you know who I am?"

I nod and motion my hand to the chair in front of me. Jessica sits down and yet I'm still speechless. Staci's last words to me were to help save Jessica from Taylor. I hadn't known she went to our school. I'm getting the feeling he likes freshman girls.

"Is it true what he did to you?" Jessica asks.

I look her straight in the eyes and nod. I'm not sure what she wants to know. Does she want me to tell her exactly what happened that night? Does she know about Staci and what he did to her too? Why am I so afraid to talk to her?

"They let him out on bail, you know," she says.

My eyes go wide. "What?" I say a little too loud. This time I see her jump. She looks scared, but I don't think he'll come after her; she didn't do anything wrong. I did. I'm the one who told on him. "What are you afraid of, Jessica?" I ask. "I don't think he's that kind of rapist. He doesn't prey on his victims." What am I some kind of expert now that I've been raped? What the hell do I know anyway?

"I know he can't hurt me now. We never were alone like you were. He just seemed so nice and sweet, but one night after a game he was upset, and it scared me so I told him I was just going to go home.

"He tried to get me in his car, saying that he'd take me home, but I went with my friend Zoey. Her mom came to get her and she lives two houses down from me so I went with them," she states. "Staci killing herself got me thinking. I mean, who would do that unless something bad had happened to them? You know, because you guys were like best friends and hung out all the time. Then, she's like, gone," Jessica wipes the tears from her face.

"I'm sorry," I say, wiping tears away myself.

We were both sitting there like a couple of crybabies, but no one is watching us because who goes to the library on their lunchbreak?

"I'm the one who's sorry because of what he did to you and Staci. I'm just glad… I mean, I'm thankful he never had the chance to make me his next victim. I'm sorry; I shouldn't have…"

I interrupt her, "Don't be." I hold up my hand. "I'm glad you…" I can't even say it. But, I feel it. "I don't want him to do this to anyone else, but I don't know how to stop him," I say because it's the truth. "I don't know if I can stop him."

"Staci told me to find you if something ever happened to her."

The skin on my forehead wrinkles, "What did you say?"

"Staci told me the day she killed herself to come find you and talk to you. She said you could help protect me from Taylor."

My dear friend since elementary is dead and yet she's still here with me, as if she'd never left.

(E)

20 | Protect The Ones You Love

After school, I go straight home, like there's any other place for me to go. Jessica and I exchanged phone numbers so we can keep in touch and let each other know if something happens related to Taylor's case.

When my mom gets home from work, I tell her about Taylor getting out on bail. Being a lawyer, she can get a restraining order issued for Taylor so he never comes around my family or me again.

I help my mom make dinner, which I never do, but I don't want to be alone in my room—not that anything could happen to me, but I don't know, it's hard to explain. My bedroom used to be my sanctuary and now after everything, being close to my family makes me feel more secure.

I think it comes down to the fact that Taylor's out there and I'm afraid he'll come after me. I don't tell my mom that, but to be honest, I think she already knows. I bet she can feel the fear rolling off me. Smell it coming out of my pores. Though, if that were true, she would've saved me weeks ago, before I tried to end my life. To stop and think about it, it could be what I did that made her open her eyes and pay more attention to me.

Once dinner is done and we all have eaten, I sit at the kitchen table doing my homework while my parents wash the dishes. I have to make-up all the work for the past three weeks.

Talk To Me

The doorbell rings and I say, "I'll get it," as I stand and make my way to the front door. Without thought, I turn the deadbolt and open the door.

I'd like to say that my life flashes before my eyes, but I didn't even have a moment to prepare myself for what happens next.

I open the door and hear the sound of a gun firing. I fall to the floor, gasping for air as I spit blood out of my mouth. This isn't how I wanted to end my life or ever pictured it would end.

Weeks ago when I hid the pills and then decided to take them, that was my decision to die and not anyone else's to make. I guess life can be funny like that. We don't always get to make the decisions we want to make, do we?

I hear my mom run into the room and she starts screaming, frantically yelling for someone to call 9-1-1, which is my dad. I can feel my sister Rosie in the room before she falls to her knees beside me, tears already streaming down her small oval face.

I can also feel *his* presence. He's still there in the doorway. When I move my eyes, I can see the shadow hovering above me as I continue to blink, trying to keep my eyes open, afraid that if they close I'd never open them again. Is he still holding the gun? Will he kill my family too? These are all questions that I ponder while fighting for my life.

I'd like to say that I remember the ambulance coming to save me. Or the police catching Taylor for shooting me, but I can't because I don't remember any of that. Once I saw Rosie beside me, everything went black…

Epilogue

Taylor Ryans wasn't arrested after shooting Carly Boyles because he turned the gun on himself before the police showed up to take him away. His body lay at their doorstep, one bullet through the right side of his head which left a small hole and nothing but half his head on the other side with part of his brain laying on their manicured lawn. He was, of course, pronounced dead at the scene.

Carly Boyles died during surgery as the surgical staff tried everything they could to stop the bleeding, but the bullet had penetrated several arteries and the bleeding wouldn't stop. She was later laid to rest in Overlook Cemetery; the same one Staci was buried in. Two best friends that had spent all their time together, died together. They were both victims of Taylor Ryans.

* * *

Taylor shooting himself showed that he was guilty of rape, not innocent. But we can't change the way some people see things or what they believe really happened. That's what makes us all different. We are who we are, and we'll see things the way we are meant to see things or how we want to see them.

As for Mick Connors, he was the one who leaked the news about Carly being raped. His mom was working at the hospital when Carly and her mom came in. With what Mick's mom told him and putting two and two together, he figured it out.

Although they seemed to be friends at the beginning, Mick turned on Carly, making everyone believe she was at fault and not the victim. Instead of being her friend and standing by her, he thrived on her weakness, but didn't have the balls to face her.

It's funny how some people pretend to be your friend, but use what they learn about you against you. Carly hadn't done anything to Mick. Maybe, that's just it. Maybe Mick liked Carly, but when he found out what happened, he thought differently of her and set out to destroy whatever was left of her.

Maybe, he still had some issues of his own to conquer. Carly mentioned that he'd cut himself before she got to know him. Who knows what really goes on in another person's mind? You can read *HELP ME!* Book-1 of the series, to get Mick's story.

If you have ever thought about suicide even once in your life, it will never venture far from your mind. There will always be a part of you that wonders, *"What if I killed myself? Does it make me a selfish person? Would life be better off without me in it?"*

We're not always prepared for these things. Some people think that it is a selfish act to commit suicide, where others may disagree. Would life be better? Not for the people who love you. Your family and friends will be the ones left after you're gone, and they will feel the pain you once carried.

* * *

Talk To Me

Rape is something that happens to many people of all genders from every race, class, and age group. Rape shouldn't happen, but it does, and we are left to face the world as if nothing has happened to us. Some of us can move past being assaulted, and others may use drugs and alcohol to ease the pain.

We even go to therapy to talk about what has happened to us, but sometimes that doesn't always help. We isolate ourselves from other people, even our friends, and especially from males because they are the most common rapists, although women are known to rape as well.

*Over eighty percent of all rape victims have some acquaintance with their attackers.

*Rape is an act of violence and control, using sex as a weapon. It is not motivated by sexual desire, but by the desire to overpower and dominate the victim.

*Rape is very traumatic and rarely does anyone lie about being raped.

*The first thing you should do is go to the emergency room.

*Call or text a family or friend, someone you feel safe with.

*If you aren't sure what to do, call a Rape Crisis Center. Search online for local numbers in your area. 1-800-656-HOPE – Rape crisis calls are anonymous and confidential.

I hope some or all of this information helps you or someone you know that has been a victim of rape. You may feel alone and that you're the only one out there who has been sexually victimized, but you're not. There are people all around us that have been sexually abused in some way, but are just too afraid, as you might be, to speak about it.

The emotional trauma caused by a sexual assault can be severe and long-lasting. You may be affected in many different ways.

Although each person is unique, there are some feelings and reactions that most sexual assault victims experience:

Fear: It is normal to feel afraid after being raped. Some people find it hard to be alone, as did Carly after coming home from *One Stepp Closer*. Towards the end, she needed to be near her family and not in her room where she once felt secure.

Anger, Loss of Control, Guilt, and Feeling Isolated: All symptoms of a survivor of rape.

However, always remember that even though many victims experience similar reactions, there are still individual differences in how people respond to the trauma of rape.

You may experience some or all of these symptoms. They may occur immediately or you may have a delayed reaction, weeks or months later. The feelings may be very intense at times. Sometimes the feelings seem to go away for a while and then come back again. Certain situations, such as seeing the assailant or testifying in court, may intensify the symptoms or cause them to recur after a period during which you have been feeling better. Like when Carly was pinned down on the sofa by Scott and re-experienced what Taylor had done to her in his car.

Everyone is different and expresses their emotions differently.

If Carly had gone to her parents when the rape happened, would she have saved her friend Staci? Would she have prevented her friend from being raped and then killing herself?

In most cases, we don't know what will happen after we've been sexually abused. We don't know what the future holds; if we did, then we could stop the bad from happening. I wish life were like that as I'm sure the person reading this book does too, but we can always dream and heal. It's a long process, however.

Author's Note: Letters at the End of Chapters

As a mother of a teen myself, I see the *word games* teenagers play in texting, tweeting, Instagram and any other new form of communication that comes down the pike. They delight in hidden clues and messages as well as coming up with the latest, greatest, creative *craze.* When I first noticed these odd letters or numbers, symbols, etc., in the short quips my teenager showed me, I was confused. *What did this mean? Should I be worried about it?*

When it was described to me as a series of interlocking letters or symbols in numerous communications to form a message, a joke, a game; and the winner was the first person to figure it out, I was intrigued. *What impressive minds our children have developed with the technology available to them!* And it's growing by leaps and bounds every day.

In this second book in the "Help Me Series", Carly's message from beyond the grave is sad and poignant:

T-A-Y-L-O-R-R-Y-A-N-S-R-A-P-E-D-M-E

Bless you, my dear fictional character. I have used my voice and my words to get your message to the "real" victims and the people who could support them, if only they knew. There are just far too many of them

out there who are never comforted, loved, or healed—who never realize their own worth. Carly wants to help as she shares her hidden secret from the very beginning of "Talk to Me".

Acknowledgements

I would like to express my many thanks and appreciation to Deborah Bowman Stevens, my editor, who loves to read these novellas about self-help. She is truly a miracle worker—my miracle worker. She patiently takes my story apart and helps me put it back together again in a way that others will understand and cherish.

She gives me such incredible, thoughtful, insightful feedback, helping me make my story an even stronger, more powerful book. I so appreciate how you also allow me to follow my heart and intuition as I edit along with you. Thank you so much for all the hard work you put into making this novella complete. I owe you so much for all you did, for all you do. Looking forward to working on my next book together.

About the Author

Donna M. Zadunajsky started out writing children's books before she accomplished and published her first novel, *Broken Promises*, in June 2012. She then has written several more novels and her first novella, *HELP ME!,* which is a subject about suicide and bullying.

She is currently working on a novel series, which she had completed three books, *Family Secrets*, *Hidden Secrets*, and *Twisted Secrets.*

More about the author go to:

http://www.donnazadunajskymalacina.blogspot.com
http://www.facebook.com/donnamzadunajsky
http://www.twitter.com/72Zadunajsky

More books by Donna M. Zadunajsky

Children's Books:

Tayla's Best Day Ever!
Tayla's Best Friend
Tayla's New Friend
Tayla goes to Grammie's House
Tayla Takes a Trip
Tayla's Day at the Beach
Tayla's First Day of School

Novels:

Broken Promises
Not Forgotten
Family Secrets 'Secrets and Second Chances' Book 1
Hidden Secrets 'Secrets and Second Chances' Book 2
Twisted Secrets 'Secrets and Second Chances' Book 3-coming 2017

Novellas:

HELP ME! – Book 1
Talk To Me – Book 2

www.ingramcontent.com/pod-product-compliance
Lightning Source LLC
Chambersburg PA
CBHW030522310726
48979CB00010B/1769/J

9781938037733